Maxwell Gray

The Silence of Dean Maitland

A Novel: Vol. I.

Maxwell Gray

The Silence of Dean Maitland
A Novel: Vol. I.

ISBN/EAN: 9783337045098

Printed in Europe, USA, Canada, Australia, Japan

Cover: Foto ©Andreas Hilbeck / pixelio.de

More available books at **www.hansebooks.com**

THE SILENCE

OF

DEAN MAITLAND

A NOVEL

BY

MAXWELL GRAY

„Denn alle Schuld rächt sich auf Erden"

IN THREE VOLUMES

VOL. I.

LONDON

KEGAN PAUL, TRENCH & CO., 1, PATERNOSTER SQUARE

1886

PART I.

"Not poppy, nor mandragora,
Nor all the drowsy syrups of the world,
Shall ever medicine thee to that sweet sleep
Which thou ow'dst yesterday."

VOL. I.

THE SILENCE

OF

DEAN MAITLAND.

———•◦•———

CHAPTER I.

THE grey afternoon was wearing on to its
chill close; the dark cope of immovable dun
cloud overhead seemed to contract and grow
closer to the silent world beneath it; and the
steep, chalky hill, leading from the ancient
village, with its hoary castle and church, up
over the bleak, barren down, was a weary
thing to climb.

The solitary traveller along that quiet
road moved her limbs more slowly, and
felt her breath coming more quickly and
shortly, as she mounted higher and higher,

and the grey Norman tower lessened and gradually sank out of sight behind her. But she toiled bravely on between the high tangled hedges, draped with great curtains of traveller's joy, now a mass of the silvery seed-feathers which the country children call " old man's beard," and variegated with the deep-purple leaves of dogwood, the crimson of briony and roseberry, the gleaming black of privet, and the gold and orange reds of ivy hangings ; and, though her pace slackened to a mere crawl, she did not pause till she reached the brow of the hill, where the hedges ceased, and the broad white high-road wound over the open down.

Here, where the enclosed land ended, was a five-barred gate in the wild hedgerow, and here the weary pedestrian, depositing the numerous parcels she carried on the ground at her feet, rested, her arms supported on the topmost bar, and her face and the upper portion of her tall figure traced clearly against the grey gloomy sky. Some linnets fluttered out of the hedge beside her, one or two silent larks sprang up from the turf of the downland sloping away from the gate, and some rooks sailed cawing overhead. All else was still with the weird, dreamy stillness that hangs over the earth on a day of chill east-wind haze.

There is a brooding expectancy about such a day that works strongly on the imagination, and suggests the dark possibilities of irresistible Fate. There is an austere poetry in the purply grey, breathless earth and the dark, unchanging sky, and a mute pathos in the quiet hush of weary Nature, thus folding her hands for rest, which has an unutterable charm for some temperaments, and touches far deeper chords than those vibrated by the brilliance and joyous tumult of life and song in the pleasant June-time. There is something of the infinite in the very monotony of the colouring; the breathless quiet, the vagueness of outline, and dimness of the all-enfolding mist are full of mystery, and invest the most commonplace objects with romance.

The sense of infinity was deepened in this

case by the vast sweep of the horizon which bounded our pedestrian's gaze. The grey fallows and wan stubble-fields sloped swiftly away from the gate to a bottom of verdant pastures dotted with trees and homesteads; beyond them were more dim fields, and then a wide belt of forest, principally of firs. To the right, the valley, in which nestled the now unseen tower of Chalkburne, widened out, bounded by gentle hills, till the stream indicating its direction became a river, on the banks of which stood the mist-veiled town of Oldport, the tall tower of whose church rose light, white, and graceful against the iron-grey sky, emulating in the glory of its maiden youth—for it had seen but two lustres—the hoary grandeur of its Norman parent at Chalkburne. Beyond the town, the river rolled on, barge-laden, to the sea, the faint blue line of which was blurred by a maze of masts where the estuary formed a harbour.

To the left of the tired gazer stretched a wide champaign, rich in woodland, and bounded in the far distance by two chalky summits, at whose steep bases surged the unseen sea, quiet to-day on the surface, but sullen with the heavy roar of the ground-swell beneath. Here and there, in the breaks of wood and forest on the horizon, Alma's accustomed eyes saw some faint grey touches which in bright summer were tiny bays of sapphire sea.

Alma Lee herself made a bright point of interest in the afternoon greyness, as she leant wearily, and not ungracefully, on the gate, her face and figure outlined clearly against the dark sky. Her dress was a bright blue, and her scarlet plaid shawl, fastened tightly about her shoulders, revealed and suggested, as only a shawl can, a full, supple form, indicative of youth and health. Her dark, thick hair was crowned by a small velvet hat, adorned with a bright bird's wing; and her dark eyes and well-formed features, reposeful and indifferent as they were at the moment, suggested latent vehemence and passion. Her hands and feet were large, the former bare, and wrapped in the gay shawl for warmth.

Alma was not thinking of the mystery and infinite possibility suggested by the grey landscape before her; still less was she dreaming of the tragic shades Fate was casting even now upon her commonplace path. Unsuspecting and innocent she stood, lost in idle thought, deaf to the steps of approaching doom, and knowing nothing of the lives that were to be so tragically entangled in the mazes of her own. Could she but have had one glimpse of the swift-coming future, with what horror would the simple country girl have started back and struggled against the first suspicion of disaster!

The silence was presently broken by four mellow, slowly falling strokes from the grey belfry of Chalkburne; then all was still again, and Alma began to pick up her parcels. Suddenly she heard the sound of hoofs and wheels, and, dropping her packages, turned once more to the gate, and appeared a very statue of contemplation by the time a dog-cart, drawn by a high-stepping chesnut, and driven by a spick-and-span groom, fair-haired and well featured, drew up beside her, and the groom sprang lightly to the ground.

" Come, Alma," he said, approaching the pensive figure, which appeared unconscious of him, " you won't say no now? You look dog-tired."

" I shall say exactly what I please, Mr. Judkins," she replied.

" Then say yes, and jump up. Chesnut is going like a bird, and will have you at Swaynestone in no time. Do say yes, do ee now."

" Thank you, I intend to walk."

" Just think what a way it is to walk to Swaynestone, and you so tired."

" I am not tired."

" Then, why are you leaning on that there gate ? "

" I am admiring the view, since you are so very inquisitive."

" Oh Lord! the view! There's a deal more view to be seen from the seat of this here cart, and it's pleasant flying along like a bird.   Come now, Alma, let me help you up."

"Mr. Judkins, will you have the kindness to drive on ? I said in Oldport that I intended to walk.   It's very hard a person mayn't do as she pleases without all this worry," replied Alma, impatiently.

"Wilful woman mun have her way," murmured the young fellow, ruefully.   "Well, let me carry them parcels home, at least."

"I intend to carry them myself, thank you.   Good afternoon;" and Alma turned her back upon the mortified youth, and appeared lost in the charms of landscape.

"Well, darn it ! if you won't come, you won't; that's flat!" the young man exclaimed angrily.   "This is your nasty pride, Miss Alma; but, mind you, pride goes before a fall," he added, springing to his perch, and sending the high-stepper flying along the level down-road like the wind, with many expressions of anger and disappointment, and sundry backward glances at Alma, who gazed with unruffled steadiness on the fields.

"I wonder," she mused, "why a person always hates a person who makes love to them? I liked Charlie Judkins well enough before he took on with this love-nonsense."

And she did not know that by declining that brief drive she had refused the one chance of escaping all the subsequent tragedy, and that her fate was even now approaching in the growing gloom.

But what is this fairy music ascending from the direction of Chalkburne, and growing clearer and louder every moment? Sweet, melodious, drowsily cheery, ring out five tiny merry peals of bells, each peal accurately matched with the other, and consisting of five tones. The music comes tumbling down in sweet confusion, peal upon peal, chime breaking into chime, in a sort of mirthful strife of melody, through all which a certain irregular rhythm is preserved, which keeps the blending harmonies from degenerating into dissonance. With a sweep and a clash and a mingling of sleepy rapture, the elfin music filled all the quiet hazy air around Alma, and inspired her with vague pleasure as she turned her head listening in the direction of the dulcet sounds, and discerned their origin in the nodding head of a large silk-coated cart-horse looming through the haze.

He was a handsome, powerful fellow, stepping firmly up the hill with the happy consciousness of doing good service which seems to animate all willing, well-behaved horses, and emerging into full view at the head of four gallant comrades, each nodding and stepping as cheerily as himself, with a ponderous waggon behind them. Each horse wore his mane in love-locks, combed over his eyes, the hair on the massive neck being tied here and there with bows of bright woollen ribbon. Each tail was carefully plaited at its spring from the powerful haunches for a few inches ; then it was tied with another bright knot, beneath which the remainder of the tail swept in untrammelled abundance almost down to the pasterns, the latter hidden by long fringes coming to the ground. The ponderous harness shone brightly on the broad, shining brown bodies, and, as each horse carried a leading-rein, thickly studded with brass bosses and fastened to the girth, and there was much polished brass about headstall, saddle, and collar, they presented a very glittering appearance.

But the crowning pride of every horse, and the source of all the music which was then witching the wintry air, was the lofty erection springing on two branching wires from every collar, and towering far above the pricked ears of the proud steeds. These wires bore a long narrow canopy placed at right angles to the horse's length, and concealing beneath a deep fringe of bright scarlet worsted the little peal of nicely graduated bells. Balls of the same bright worsted studded the roof of the little canopy, and finished the gay trappings of the sturdy rustics, who bore these accumulated honours with a sort of meek rapture.

The waggon these stout fellows drew needed all their bone and sinew to bring it up and down the steep, hilly roads. Its hind-wheels were as high as Alma's head; their massive felloes, shod with double tires, were a foot broad ; the naves were like moderate-sized casks. High over the great hind wheels arched the waggon's ledge in a grand sweep, descending with a boat-like curve to the smaller front wheels, whence it rose again, ending high over the wheeler's haunches, like the prow of some old ship over the sea. A massive thing of solid timber it was, with blue wheels and red body, slightly toned by weather. On the front, in red letters on a yellow ground, was painted, " Richard Long, Malbourne, 1860."

Two human beings, who interrupted the fairy music with strange gutturals and wild ejaculations to the steeds, mingled with sharp whip-cracks, accompanied this imposing equipage. One was a tall, straight-limbed man in fustian jacket and trousers, a coat slung hussar-wise from his left shoulder, and a cap worn slightly to one side, with a pink chrysanthemum stuck in it. His sunburnt face was almost the hue of his yellow-brown curls and short beard ; his eyes were blue ;

and his strong, laboured gait resembled that
of his horses.   The other was a beardless lad,
his satellite, similarly arrayed, minus the
flower.   Sparks flew from the road when the
iron hoofs and heavy iron boots struck an
occasional flint.   When the great waggon
was fairly landed on the brow of the hill, the
horses were brought to by means of sundry
strange sounds and violent gestures on the
part of the men, and, with creaking and
groaning and halloing, the great land-ship
came to anchor, the elfin chimes dropped into
silence, interrupted by little bursts of melody
at every movement of the horses, and the lad
seized a great wooden mallet and thrust
beneath the hind wheel.   The carter leant
placidly against the ponderous shaft with his
face to Alma, and struck a match to kindle
his replenished pipe.

"Coldish," he observed, glancing with
surly indifference towards her.

"It is cold," returned Alma, drawing her
shawl cosily round her graceful shoulders;
while the wheeler, stimulated into curiosity

by his master's voice, turned round to look at
Alma, and shook out a little peal of bells,
which roused the emulation of his four
brothers, who each shook out a little chime
on his own account; while the waggoner
glanced slowly round the vast horizon, and,
after some contemplation, said in a low,
bucolic drawl—

"Gwine to hrain, I 'lows."

"It looks like it," replied Alma. "How is
your wife, William?"

The waggoner again interrogated the
horizon for inspiration, and, after some
thought, answered with a jerk, "Neuce the
same."

"I hope she will soon be about again," said
Alma; and the leader emphasized her words
by shaking a little music from his canopy,
and thus stimulated his brothers to do like-
wise. "You come home lighter than you set
out," she added, looking at the nearly empty
waggon, which she had seen pass in the
morning filled with straw.

William turned slowly round and gazed

inquiringly at the waggon, as if struck by a new idea, for some moments; then he said, "Ay." After this he looked thoughtfully at Alma and her parcels for some moments, until his soul again found expression in the words, "Like a lift?" the vague meaning of which was elucidated by the pointing of his whip towards the waggon.

Alma assented, and with the waggoner's assistance soon found herself, with all her merchandise, comfortably installed in the great waggon, which was empty save for a few household and farming necessaries from Oldport. Before mounting—a feat, by the way, not unworthy of a gymnast—she stroked the wheel horse's thick silken coat admiringly.

"You do take care of your horses at Malbourne, William," she said. "I heard father say this morning he never saw a better-groomed and handsomer team than yours."

William went on silently arranging Alma's seat, and stowing her parcels for her; but a smile dawned at the corners of his mouth,

and gradually spread itself over the whole of
his face, and his pleasure at length found a
vent, when he reached the ground, in a sound-
ing thwack of his broad hand on the wheeler's
massive flank—a thwack that set the bells
a-tremble on the horse's neck, and sent a
sympathetic shiver of music through all the
emulous brotherhood.

"Ay," he observed, with a broad smile of
admiration along the line of softly swaying
tails and gently moving heads, with their
nostrils steaming in the cold air; "he med
well say that."

"Ay," echoed Jem, the satellite, removing
the sledge mallet from the wheel and striding
to the front, with a reflection of his chief's
pleasure in his ruddy face as he glanced
affectionately at the team, "that he med."

It was not Alma's admiration which
evoked such satisfaction—she was but a
woman, and naturally could not tell a good
horse from a donkey; but her father, Ben
Lee, Sir Lionel Swaynestone's coachman, a
man who had breathed the air of stables

from his cradle, and who drove the splendid silk-coated, silver-harnessed steeds in the Swaynestone carriages, his opinion was something. With a joyous crack of the whip, and a strange sound from the recesses of his throat, William bid his team " Gee-up ! "

The mighty hoofs took hold of the road, the great wheels slowly turned, a shower of confused harmony fell in dropping sweetness from the bells, and with creaking and groaning, and nodding heads, and rhythmic blending of paces and music, the waggon lumbered ponderously along the level chalk road which led, unenclosed by hedge or fence, over the open down.

To ride in a waggon with ease, and at the same time enjoy the surrounding landscape without a constant exercise of gymnastic skill in balancing and counter-balancing the body in response to the heavy swaying and jerking of the unwieldy machine, is difficult; to sit on the ledge is to be an acrobat; to lie on the floor is to see nothing but sky, besides having one's members violently wrenched one from the other. Alma, however, was very comfortably placed on a pile of sacks, which served as an arm-chair, deadened the jerking power of the motion, and left her head and shoulders above the ledge, so that she could well see the grey surrounding landscape in the deepening haze.

She leant back with a feeling of agreeable languor, wrapped her hands in her shawl, and gazed dreamily on the down rising steeply to the left, and forming, where chalk had been quarried in one place, a miniature precipice, crested with overhanging copse, rich in spring with fairy treasures of violets in white sheets over the moss, clusters of primroses and oxlips among the hazel stumps, blue lakes of hyacinth, and waving forests of anemone; and she gazed on the sloping fields, farmsteads, and bounding forest to the right, lulled by the steady music of the bells, among which she heard from time to time William's satisfied growl of " Ay, he med well say that," and the occasional song of Jem, as he trudged along by the leader—

" For to plough, and to sow, and to reap, and to mow,
Is the work of the farmer's bu-oy-oy."

Happy and harmless she looked in her
rustic chariot, as they rolled slowly along in
the gathering gloom, now over a heathy
stretch nearly at the summit of the down,
past a lonely, steep-roofed, red-tiled hostelry,
with a forge cheerily glowing by its side,
whence the anvil-music rose and blended
pleasantly with that of the bell-team, and
over which hung a sign-board bearing the
blacksmith's arms, the hammer, with the
couplet inscribed beneath, " By hammer and
hand, All arts do stand."

Downhill now, with the heavy drag cast
beneath the wheel by mighty efforts on the
part of Jem; then again on the level road,
with the chalk down always rising to the left,
and falling away to the right; past farm-
houses, where the cattle stood grouped in the
yard and the ducks quacked for their evening
meal; then once more down a hill, steep and
difficult, down to the level of a willow-shaded
stream by a copse, outside which daffodils

rioted all over the sloping lea descending to
the brookside in spring; and then again up
and up, with straining and panting and creaking, with iron feet pointed into and gripping
the steep chalk road, with louder pealing of
the fairy chimes, whose rhythm grows irregular and fitful, with strange shouts and
gestures from the men, with " Whup! " and
" Whoa! " and " Hither! " with many pauses,
when the great heads droop, the music stops,
and the mallet is brought into requisition.

Happy and harmless indeed was Alma, the
lashes drooping over her rose-leaf cheeks, her
fancies roving unfettered. She was hoping
to get home betimes, for she had something
nice for father's tea among her parcels, and
she was thinking of the penny periodical
folded up in her basket, and wondering how
the heroine was getting on in the story which
broke off abruptly at such an interesting
moment in the last number. Was the peasant
girl, in whom Alma detected a striking like
ness to herself, really going to marry the poor
young viscount who was so deplorably in

love with her ?　She could not help furnishing the viscount with the form and features
of Mr. Ingram Swaynestone, Sir Lionel's
eldest son, though the latter was fair, while
the viscount happened to be dark.

Now they are at the summit of the steep
hill, and pause to breathe and replenish
pipes.　On one side is dense coppice ; on the
other, Swaynestone Park slopes down in
woodland, glade, and park-like meadow to the
sea-bounded horizon.　Then on again, up hill
and down dale, past cottage and farmstead,
with the park always sloping away to the
sea on the right.　Lights glow cheerily now
from distant cottage windows, and they can
even catch glimpses of lights from the façade
of Swaynestone House between the trees occasionally, while the merry music peals on in
its drowsy rhythm, and little showers of
sparks rise at the contact of iron-shod wheel
and foot with the flinty road.

They have just passed the entrance-gates of
Swaynestone—lonely gates, unfurnished with
a lodge—and the waggon stops with inter-

rupted music at some smaller gates on the
other side of the road, where the upland still
rises, not in bare down, but in rich meadow, to
a hanging wood, out of which peeps dimly in
the dusk a small white structure, built with a
colonnade supporting an architrave, to imitate
a Greek temple—Alma's home.

"Ay! he med well say that," repeated the
waggoner, still digesting the pleasure of
Ben Lee's compliment, and slapping the
wheel-horse's vast flank, so that the fairy
chime began again, and the smack resounded
like an accompaniment to its music. It was
fairly dark in the road; the misty dusk of
evening was overshadowed by the thick belt
of chestnut, lime, and beech bounding the
park by the roadside; and the large horn
lantern was handed to Alma to aid her in
gathering her parcels together, and its light
fell upon her bright dark eyes, and rosy,
dimpled cheeks, making her appear more
than ever as if her gaudy dress was but a
disguise assumed for a frolic. Her almond-
shaped, rather melancholy eyes sparkled as

she looked in the young carter's stolid face, and thanked him heartily.

"I have had such a nice ride," she added pleasantly, and the horses one by one dropped a bell-note or two to emphasize her words.

"You must gie I a toll for this yere ride," returned William, with a look of undisguised, but not rude admiration.

Alma flushed, and drew back. "How much do you want?" she asked, taking out her purse, and pretending not to understand.

"You put that there in your pocket," he replied, offended, "and gie I a kiss."

"Indeed, I shall do nothing of the kind," retorted Alma. "Let me get down. I'll never ride with you again, if I walk till I drop—that I won't."

But the waggoner insisted on his toll, and vowed that she should not descend till it was paid; and poor Alma protested and stormed vainly, whilst Jem leaned up against a horse and laughed, and adjured her to make haste. Alma burst into tears, wrung her hands, and wished that she had not been so obdurate to poor Charlie Judkins. He would not have been so rude, she knew. Nor, indeed, would William have been so persistent had she not offended him by her unlucky offer of money, and roused the dogged obstinacy of his class. She darted to the other side of the waggon, but in vain ; William was too quick, and she was just on the point of raising her voice, in the hope that her father might be near, when a light, firm step was heard issuing from the park gates, and a clear and singularly musical voice broke into the dispute with a tone of anthority.

"For shame, William Grove!" it said. "How can you be so cowardly ? Let the girl go directly. Why, it is Alma Lee, surely!"

CHAPTER II.

THE speaker emerged into the little circle of
light cast by the lantern—a slight, well-built,
youthful figure of middle height yet commanding presence, clad in dark grey, with
a round, black straw hat and a neat white
necktie, the frequent costume of a country
curate in those days, when the clerical garb
had not reached so high a stage of evolution
as at present. His beardless face made him
look still younger than he really was; his
features were refined and clearly cut; his hair
very dark; and his eyes, the most striking
feature of his face, were of that rare, dazzling
light blue which can only be compared to
a cloudless, noon sky in June, when the pale,
intense blue seems penetrated to overflowing
with floods of vivid light.

"I waren't doing no harm," returned the waggoner, with a kind of surly respect; "I gied she a ride, and she med so well gie I a kiss."

"And you a married man!" cried the indignant young deacon; "for shame!"

"There ain't no harm in a kiss," growled William, with a sheepish, discomfited look, while he stood aside and suffered the new-comer to help Alma in her descent.

"There is great harm in insulting a respectable young woman, and taking advantage of her weakness. As for a kiss, it is not a seemly thing between young people who have no claim on each other, though there may be no positive harm in it. You ought to know better, William."

"There ain't no harm for the likes of we," persisted the waggoner. "'Tain't as though Alma was a lady; she's only a poor man's daughter."

"And a poor man's daughter has as much right to men's respect as a duchess," cried the young fellow, with animation. "I wonder

you can say such a thing, Grove. And
you a poor man yourself, with a little
daughter of your own! How would you
like her to be kissed against her will?"

William muttered to the effect that "Anybody med kiss she"—which was true enough,
as she had seen but three summers yet—and
went on twining his whip with a cowed,
injured look, while Alma gazed in awed
admiration at her handsome young champion,
whose kindling eyes seemed to send forth
floods of pale-blue light in the gloom.

"There is something so unmanly in at-
tacking a girl's self-respect," continued the
eager champion. "I did not think you
capable of it, William. A stout fellow like
you, a man I always liked. Go home to
your wife, and think better of it. I will see
you across the meadow myself, Alma, though
it is hard that a girl cannot be abroad alone
at this hour."

So saying, the young Bayard possessed
himself of sundry of Alma's parcels, and
with a pleasant "Good night, Jem," turned

his back on the waggon and opened the gate, through which Alma passed quickly, followed by her protector, while the cumbrous waggon went on its way to the rhythmic jangle of the sweetly clashing bells, and William trudged stolidly on with his accustomed whip-crackings and guttural exclamations, murmuring from time to time with a mortified air, "There ain't no harm in a kiss!" And, indeed, he meant no harm, though he took care not to relate the incident to his wife; it was only his rough tribute to Alma's unaccustomed beauty, and signified no more than a gracefully turned allusion in higher circles. "And Mr. Cyril must go a-spiling of she," he added, "as though she didn't look too high already. But pride goes before a fall, as I've heerd 'un zay." Ominous repetition of Judkins's words!

Alma, in the mean time, murmured her thanks to her chivalrous protector, and stepped up the dewy meadow with a beating breast and a flushing cheek, her ears tingling with the words, "A poor man's daughter has

as much right to respect as a duchess," her
heart swelling at the memory of the courtesy
with which Maitland handed her down from
the waggon and carried half her parcels; she
knew that a veritable duchess would not
have been treated with more honour. All
her life she had known Cyril Maitland. She
had sported with him over that very lea,
where the tall yellow cowslips nodded in
spring, and where they had pelted each other
with sweet, heavy cowslip-balls; she had
kissed and cuffed him many a time, though
he was always " Master Cyril " to the coachman's child; and, as they grew up, had been
inclined to discuss him with a half-respectful,
half-familiar disparagement, such as well-
known objects receive. Never till that fatal
evening had his grace of mind and person
and the singular charm of his manner keenly
touched her. But when he stood there in
the lantern's dim rays, looking so handsome
and so animated by the impulsive chivalry
with which he defended her, and she heard
the musical tones and refined accents of the

voice pleading her cause and the cause of
her sex and her class, a new spirit came to
her—a spirit of sweetness and of terror,
which set all her nerves quivering, and
opened a new world of wonder and beauty
to her entranced gaze. As holy as a young
archangel, and as beautiful, he seemed to the
simple girl's dazzled thoughts, and she felt
that no harm could ever come to her in that
charmed presence, no pain ever touch her.

All unconscious of the tumult of half-
conscious emotion awakening beside him,
Cyril Maitland walked on, chatting with
pleasant ease on all sorts of homely topics,
in no wise surprised at his companion's faltering, incoherent replies, which he attributed
to the embarrassment from which he had just
delivered her. The dulcet clashing of the bells
grew fainter, and then rose on a sudden gust
of wind just as they reached the door of the
strangely built white house, before the square
windows of which rose a small colonnade of
white pillars. Alma opened the door, and a
ruddy glow rushed out upon her, while

within a cheerful little home-scene presented
itself. A small table, covered with a clean
white cloth, touched with rose by the firelight,
and spread with tea-things, was drawn up
before the glowing hearth, and a warm aroma
of tea and toast greeted the tired, hungry
girl. Before the fire sat a strong, middle-
aged man in an undress livery, consisting
partly of a sleeved waistcoat, busily engaged
in making toast; while a neatly dressed woman
moved about the warm parlour, adding a few
touches to the table.

"Just in time, Alma," called out the man,
without turning his head.

"And a pretty time, too," added the
woman, who was Alma's stepmother. "Why
hadn't you a come along with Charlie Judkins
this hour agone ? Gadding about till it's
dark night—— Oh, Mr. Cyril, I beg your
pardon, sir!" and she dropped a curtsey,
while her husband turned, and rose.

"May I come in ?" asked Cyril, pausing,
hat in hand, and smiling his genial smile.
" Your tea is very tempting, Mrs. Lee."

"Come in and welcome, Master Cyril," said the coachman, as Cyril, with the air of an accustomed guest, placed his hat on a side-table adorned with the family Bible, workboxes, and tea-trays, and took the chair Mrs. Lee handed him.

"Why, I've not had tea with you for an age," continued Cyril, stroking a large tabby cat, which sprang purring upon his knee the moment he was seated ; "and I don't deserve any now, since I come straight from the drawing-room at Swaynestone, where the rites of the teapot were being celebrated. But the ladies there have no idea of tea-making, and I only had two cups, and was tantalized with a vague sketch of a piece of bread and butter."

"Well, you always were a rare one for tea, Master Cyril," returned his hostess. "If I had but known you were coming, I'd 'a made some of them hot cakes. But there's jam in plenty, some blackberry as Alma made this fall."

"Alma came by Long's waggon," he explained, when she had withdrawn to lay aside her hat and shawl; "and as I chanced to be at the gate when she got down, I saw her across the meadow."

"Thank 'ee kindly, Master Cyril. I don't like her to be out alone at nights," said Ben Lee, "though, to be sure, there's only our own people about on the estate."

Before Alma's mind there arose a vision of the Swaynestone drawing-room as she had seen it once at tea-time when she was summoned to speak to the young ladies about some needlework she was doing for them. She saw in imagination the long range of windows with their rich curtains; the mirrors and couches; the cabinets filled with rare and costly *bric-à-brac*; the statuettes and pictures; the painted ceiling of the long, lofty room; the beautiful chimneypiece of sculptured Parian marble; the rich glow from the hearth throwing all kinds of warm reflections upon the splendid apartment, and principally upon the little table, laden with silver and priceless china, by the fire; and the charming

group of ladies in their stylish dress and
patrician beauty, half seen in the fire-lit
dusk. It was a world of splendour to
Alma's unaccustomed eyes—a place in which
an ordinary mortal could in no wise sit down
with any comfort, without, indeed, a something almost amounting to sacrilege; a world
in which the perfume of hot-house flowers
took away the bated breath, and in which no
footfall dared echo, where voices were low
and musical, and manners full of courteous
ease; a world inhabited by beings untouched
by common cares, with other thoughts, and
softer, more beautifully adorned lives; a world
which Alma entered with a burdensome sense
of being out of place, in which she only
spoke when spoken to, and where she heard
herself discussed as if she were a thing
without hearing.

" What! is this Lee's daughter ? " Lady
Swaynestone had asked, putting up her gold-
rimmed glasses, and taking a quiet survey of
Alma and her blushes.

" Surely you remember little Alma Lee,

mother," Ethel Swaynestone replied. " She
has shot up, you see, like the rest of us."

" Ah, to be sure! How the time goes,
Ethel! How is your mother, Alma? And
she is embroidering Maude's handkerchiefs ?
A very nice employment for a young woman.
But I don't like her gown; it is far too
smart for a coachman's daughter."

" Nonsense, mother dear. Why shouldn't
she be smart, if she likes ? But if you want
really to look nice, Alma, you must not wear
violet and pale blue together," said the fair-
haired Maude, with a sweet look of interest
in Alma's appearance that won her heart,
wounded as it was by " her ladyship's " want
of consideration.

Very glad was Alma to retire from that
august presence—almost as glad as she had
been to enter it. And Mr. Cyril had walked
straight from the splendid apartment, from
the light of Miss Ethel and Miss Maude's
eyes, and the sound of their sweet, cultured
voices, with a disparaging remark upon their
tea, and chosen Alma's own humble everyday

dwelling and homely meal in the narrow room in preference. This filled her with a strange, indefinable emotion, half pleasure and half pain. Some instinct told her that he was the same welcomed, admired guest there as here ; that he spoke with the same easy charm to Lady Swaynestone and her daughters and the high-born visitors he chanced to meet there as to her parents and herself. And could her imagination have borne her into Cyril's future, she would have seen him, as he subsequently was, a welcomed frequent guest at royal tables, where his beautiful voice and perfect manner cast the same glamour over the palace atmosphere as over that of the coachman's little dwelling.

Quickly as Alma returned to the parlour, she yet found time to arrange her rich hair and add a necklace of amber beads, thus imparting a kind of gipsy splendour to her dark face, and other little trifles to her dress ; and very handsome she looked in the fire-light—for the one candle but emphasized the gloom—with that new sparkle in her eyes and flush on her cheek. It was Cyril who recommended her to toast the sausages she had brought from Oldport instead of frying them; he and Lilian had often cooked them so in the schoolroom at home, he said, when Mrs. Lee demurred at trusting to his culinary skill. It was Cyril also who suggested the agreeable addition of cold potatoes warmed up.

"Well, Master Cyril, I never thought to see you teach my wife cooking," laughed Ben, paying a practical compliment to his skill. "Hand Master Cyril some tea, Alma; and do you taste the sausages, my girl. Why, where's your appetite after tramping all the way into Oldport, and nothing but a bit of bread and cheese since breakfast? You shan't walk there and back again any more; that and the shopping is too much. And so you came along part of the way in Long's waggon, when you might have been tooled along by the best horse in our stables, and Judkins fit to cry about it. Now, don't you call that silly, Mr. Cyril?"

"Every one to his taste, Ben. I prefer the dog-cart."

"And it ain't every day a girl like Alma gets a chance of riding behind such a horse or beside such a young man," added Mrs. Lee, severely. "But there's people as never knows where their bread's buttered."

"There are people," said Alma, with a toss of her graceful head, "as know what they've a mind to do, and do it."

"And there's headstrong girls as lives to repent," retorted the stepmother.

"Ay, you was always a wilful one, Alma," said her father; "but if you don't look out you'll be a old maid, and you won't like that. And a smarter fellow than Charlie Judkins never crossed a horse. No drink with Charlie—goes to church regular, and has a matter of fifty pound in the bank, and puts by every week. And Sir Lionel ready to find him a cottage and raise his wages when he marries."

"Well, let him marry, then," returned Alma, airily; "*I* don't want to prevent him.

I dare say Mr. Cyril would be kind enough to perform the ceremony, if he wished it."

"I should have the greatest pleasure, Alma, particularly if he chose a certain friend of mine. For, as your father says, Charlie is a really good fellow, as warmhearted a man as I know, and deserves a good wife."

"There are plenty of good wives to be had," returned Alma; "no doubt Mr. Judkins will soon find one, especially as he has so many friends to put in a word for him."

"Ay, and he might have the pick of girls in Malbourne, and five miles round," added Mrs. Lee.

"And Charlie won't stand Alma's hoity-toity airs much longer," chimed in her father. "He was terrible angry this afternoon, and talked about stuck-up faggots, he did. And you rising twenty-two, and refused Mr. Ingram's own man. I don't know what 'd be good enough for ye, Alma, I don't, without 'twas Mr. Ingram hisself. Ain't she a wilful one, Mr. Cyril ?"

"We mustn't be hard upon her, Ben. She has a right to refuse a man if she doesn't care for him. But any girl might think twice before refusing Charlie Judkins," said Cyril, in his gentle, gracious way. "I was to tell you, Mrs. Lee," he added, "that we are running short of eggs at the Rectory, and ask if your fowls were laying enough to spare?"

"Ourn have mostly give over laying, but Mrs. Maitland shall have a dozen so soon as Alma can get over to-morrow. Why, you don't bide at the Rectory now, sir?"

"No. I have rooms in my own parish at Shotover," he replied; "but I am always running in and out at home. It is only a mile and a half, you know; and Shotover is such a tiny parish, it leaves us very idle."

"That's well for your book-learning, Mr. Cyril. I reckon you have to know a good deal more before you can be priested next Trinity. When are ye coming over to Malbourne to preach to we?"

"Oh, not for a long while, Ben. I feel as

if I could never have the assurance to preach
to all you grave and reverend seigniors.   I
don't even preach at Shotover, if I can help
it," he replied, with an air of ingenuous
modesty that became him well.

"You mun get over that, sir," continued
Ben; "you mun think of Timothy.   He
was to let no man despise his youth, you
mind."

"Certainly, Ben.   But I have only been
ordained three months, and I may well hold
my tongue till I have learned a little wisdom.
Ah, Ben, you can't imagine what a dreadful
ordeal it is to preach one's first sermon!   I
feel cold water running down my back when
I think of it.   They say my face was whiter
than my surplice, and my voice sounded so
loud and strange in my ears I thought it
must frighten people, instead of which they
could scarcely hear me."

"Lauk-a-mercy, Mr. Cyril, you'll soon get
over that," said Mrs. Lee, in a tone of consolation.   "That's just how I felt the first
time I acted parlourmaid, Jane being took

ill, and a party to dinner, and I housemaid.
You mid 'a seen the glasses knock up agen
the decanter when I filled them, the jellies
all a-tremble with the palpitations—not to
mention the first time I walked into Malbourne Church with Lee, and made sure I
should a dropped every step I took up the
aisle, and all them boys staring, and your pa
beginning 'the wicked man.' But law! I
thinks nothing of it now."

"You may still hear my teeth chatter in
Shotover Church, nevertheless, Mrs. Lee,"
replied Cyril, softly stroking the cat, which
still nestled purring on his knee, and casting
an amused glance on Mrs. Lee and on Alma,
whose face expressed the most sympathetic
interest. "But, as you say, I shall get over
it in time. And, indeed, if the congregation consisted of Alma, and Lilian, and
Mr. Ingram Swaynestone, and his sisters,
I shouldn't mind preaching at Malbourne.
Fellow-sinners of my own age are not
so appalling."

"Ay, with a head like yourn, you med be

a bishop some day," observed Lee, thoughtfully. " What's this yere thing they made
ye at college? somat to do with quarrelling?"

" A wrangler."

" Ah! You may depend upon it, it's a fine
thing to be a wrangler. Mr. Ingram, now,
they only made he a rustic; but he was at
t'other place—Oxford, they calls it."

" He was rusticated," said Cyril, gravely.
" That is not so advantageous as being made
a wrangler."

" You see, I was right, after all, mother,"
Alma interposed; "and you always would
have it that Mr. Cyril was a mangler. As
if they had mangles at Cambridge!"

" You'd better be less forward with your
tongue, and get on with your vittles, miss.
Why, bless the girl, she's eat nothing, and
if that ain't the third time she've put sugar
into the milk-jug by mistake! Why, father,
whatever's come to her?"

Alma blushed prettily, but her confusion
almost amounted to distress; and Cyril, with
his ready tact, again drew attention from her.

"You must not imagine," he said, "that I have to pass my time in strife and dissension because I am a wrangler. Quite the contrary. Thank you for the tea, Mrs. Lee. Good night, Ben;" and, placing the cat very gently on the warm hearth, and shaking hands with his hosts, Cyril rose, took his hat, and followed Alma out into the darkness.

She bore the candle, and by its light guided him to the little wicket at the end of the garden, where, with a curtsey, she bid him good night.

"Good night, Alma," he returned carelessly, and stepped briskly down the dark meadow, the grass of which was crisped now by frost; while Alma remained at the wicket, that he might have the benefit of the candle's feeble ray.

When he was half-way across, he suddenly stopped and turned.

"Oh, Alma!" he cried, retracing his steps, when she looked up with startled inquiry in his face, "I quite forgot the very thing I came for." Here he paused, overcome with

surprise at the vivid, tense expression of
Alma's bright face, and a ray of illumination
shot over the something he had observed in
the house, the absent manner and the lack of
appetite, and accounted for her disparagement
of the enamoured Judkins. By these signs
he knew that Alma was in love with some
other swain. "I quite forgot Miss Lilian's
message to you. My sister is getting up a
Bible-class for young women, and she wishes
you to join. She is to hold it in her room
at the Rectory after evensong on Sunday
afternoons. Will you come?"

"Oh, I don't know, Mr. Cyril! You see,
I should be dark home these winter nights,"
returned Alma, hesitating and blushing, and
looking up at Cyril and down on the frosted
grass and up again.

"Well, you can talk it over with Miss
Lilian when you bring the eggs. I think we
might get over the difficulty of getting home
in the dark. If that was all, I might see
you home myself."

"Oh, Mr. Cyril!"

There was a quiver and flash and illumination in the words and look of the simple, unconscious girl which shot like electric flame through her interlocutor's frame, and made him speechless. The blue radiance from his eyes mingled for a moment with the dark fire of Alma's, and a strange, unaccustomed tremor, that was not all pain, set his pulses beating as they were not used to beat, and stirred all the currents of his blood.

"Good night, Alma," he said shortly, and in a voice so unlike his own that the girl stood petrified in pained amazement; and he turned, and sped swiftly over the crisp grass to the gate, glad to be out of the influence of the solitary candle's dim light.

He let the gate fall-to with a clash which made it vibrate backwards and forwards for some minutes before it found rest, and strode rapidly over the dark highway beneath the trees.

"What have I done?" he muttered, with a beating heart. "Oh, my God! I meant no harm. What have I done?"

Yet the warm, delicious glow still lingered,
paining him, in his breast, and he strode on
with his head bent down, humbled and
wretched. His soul was yet spotless as the
untrodden snow; all his hopes and tastes
were innocent; the fierce flame of temptation
had never yet cast its scorching glare upon
him, hitherto he had deemed himself in-
vulnerable. In his trouble, he put his hand
instinctively in his pockets, where nestled as
usual the rubbed covers of his " Visitations
and Prayers for the Sick," and other devo-
tional books, and was comforted. He lifted
his head, and felt in his breast-pocket for a
letter, the pressure of which, though he could
not read it beneath that dark dome of solid
night, fully restored the serenity to his face.
It began, " Dearest Cyril," and ended, " Ever
affectionately yours, Marion Everard;" it
alluded to the pains of separation, and the
hopes expressed by Cyril of a possible
marriage in a year's time.

They had been engaged a whole year,
and the necessity of waiting another year

before marriage was the tragedy of their young lives. A year seemed an eternity to them, and the life they passed apart from each other no life. A vision of Marion's gentle face brightened the curtain of thick darkness spread before Cyril. He recalled her tones and looks with a rush of sweet affection—all the tender looks she had ever given him, and they were many; but he could not recall any one look that resembled the glance of fervid, unquenchable passion which flashed from Alma's tell-tale eyes in that fatal moment at the gate. Such a look he had beheld in no woman's eyes; such a look, he feared, in the narrowness of his serene purity, could light no good woman's eyes.

He was wrong. The flame which burnt in poor, innocent Alma's breast, and which her guileless nature so rashly and unconsciously betrayed, descended like a celestial glory upon her life with a purifying and strengthening power, which could have lifted her to unimagined summits of heroism.

There are people whose lives are never touched by passion, and who, when they come in contact with it, recognize only its strength, which they dread, and condemn its mysteries as baleful. Such was Cyril in these white young days of his before any shadow fell upon his sunny, safe path. Such was not Cyril in after-days, when the agony of the penitent and the evildoer found a responsive echo in his heart, and made him pitiful and lenient in judging character and discriminating motives. But to-night, in spite of the momentary glow for which he so despised himself, he drew the robe of the Pharisee about his upright soul, and cast a stone of condemnation upon the sufferer as he passed her swiftly by.

Alma remained statue-like, with her solitary light painting a feeble halo on the all-encompassing gloom, until Cyril's steps had ceased to echo along the lonely highway, and her mother called to her to bring back the candle and shut the door.

As soon as she had obeyed, she found a

pretext for going to her room, and there, sitting down on the edge of the bed in the dark, she burst into tears.

"I am tired, and William Grove frightened me," she said to herself; and a few minutes later she was at needlework in the parlour, singing like any wild bird.

CHAPTER III.

A WARM glimmer of ruddy light on the thick
darkness told Cyril of the approach of the
wheelwright's house and shop, and, passing
this and descending the hill, he became aware
of the rich crimson which marked the lower
windows of the Sun Inn, and found himself
at the end of the wheelwright's yard, at the
meeting of four roads. Opposite the Sun,
and coloured by its light, a sign-post reared
itself at the corner, oblique, and appearing to
gesticulate madly with its outspread arms.
This corner turned, all the village sparkled
out in a little constellation of cottage case-
ments before his gaze; and there, beyond the
brook, which murmured faintly in the stillness,
the Rectory windows shone out among masses
of foliage, or rather of branches, behind which

the grey church spire lifted itself unseen in the mirk. As soon as Cyril's foot was within the gate, a sudden illumination from the hall door, which simultaneously opened, poured itself upon the drive, and showed him the outline of a woman's young and graceful figure in the porch.

"Did you hear me coming, Lilian?" asked he, entering the house. "Your hearing must indeed be acute."

"Did we hear him, Mark Antony?" echoed Lilian, addressing a magnificent black cat, with white breast and paws, which had been sitting upon the step at her feet, and gazing with grave expectancy down the drive till Cyril reached the door, when he rose, and respectfully greeted him with elevated tail and gentle mews, interspersed with purring. "You know that puss and I have an extra sense, which tells us when you are coming," she replied lightly, as she passed her arm through his, and led him through the little hall into the drawing-room, on the threshold of which a terrier and a pug sprang out to greet the new-comer with short barks of joy and sudden bounds and various wild expressions of delight—an indiscreet behaviour, quietly rebuked 'by two swift but dignified strokes of Mark Antony's white velvet paw, which sent the heedless animals, with dismal yelps and mortified tails, to a respectful distance.

A lady lay on a sofa near the fire, and a boy and a girl of some eight and nine years rolled on the hearthrug with some toys. These children, with Cyril and Lilian, who were twins, constituted the sole remainder of Mrs. Maitland's once too numerous family. What with bearing and rearing them all, and the sorrow of losing so many, her strength was now exhausted, and the prime of her life was passed chiefly on that sofa, among its warm rugs. Cyril bent to kiss her, and a look of pride and joy lighted her pale, refined face as she gazed upon him.

The children sprang upon Cyril, and he, having caressed them, took a seat by Lilian, who was at the writing-table, from which she had risen on his approach.

" Will it do ? " he asked, gazing upon some manuscript before her.

" I think so," she replied. " I have drawn a line through the most ornate passages. But you must really try and adapt yourself to your congregation, Cyril. This goes completely over their heads. Be less elaborate, and speak from your heart, simply and honestly."

"The discipline which turns out wranglers," observed Cyril, with a dry little smile, " does not train popular rustic preachers."

" Cyril's sermons again ? " asked Mrs. Maitland.   " Lilian should compose them entirely, I think.   And yet I am wrong, for I doubt if either of you could do anything without the other."

The twins smiled, knowing this to be perfectly true. They were alike, and yet different. Lilian's features were fuller than Cyril's ; her eyes softer and of a grey colour, but they met the gazer with an even more powerful electric thrill than Cyril's light blue orbs ; her hair was many shades lighter than

her brother's; and while Cyril could not
appear in any assembly without exciting
interest and drawing all eyes to himself,
Lilian had a peculiar manner of pervading
places without attracting the slightest observation. Gradually one became aware of an influence, and only after a long time discovered
the personage from whom it emanated.

No one ever praised Lilian's beauty, though
she possessed all the elements of loveliness.
She shared Cyril's musical voice, but lacked its
more powerful and penetrating tones. Cyril
had beautifully shaped hands, but Lilian's
were like two fair spirits, and formed the
only striking part of her personality; they
were the first thing the stranger observed in
her, and, once observed, they were never for
a moment forgotten. The twins had shared
everything from their babyhood. The same
tutor demanded equal tasks of brother and
sister; and when Cambridge separated them,
Lilian still followed the course of her brother's
studies, and would doubtless have been a high
wrangler, had she been submitted to the same

tests as he. The peculiar bond between them was respected and acknowledged even by Mark Antony, who was, as his mistress frequently observed, a cat of considerable force of character. Besides Lilian, Cyril was the only human being Mark Antony ever followed or fawned upon, and it was supposed that his very strong affections were entirely bestowed upon the twins.

To strangers this cat was haughtily indifferent; and, if a visitor took such a liberty as to stroke his ebon fur, would rise and walk away with offended majesty. To the family he observed a distant but eminently courteous demeanour; to the servants he was condescending; to the children polite, but never familiar, their respectful caresses being received with dignified resignation, and never suffered to go beyond a certain point; his bearing to the dogs was that of a despot. He was a great warrior, and suffered no other cat to intrude so much as a paw on the Rectory grounds; hence his name.

He never left Lilian while she was in the house, and at certain seasons exacted games of play from her, scorning to play with any one else, save occasionally when he unbent so far as to entangle himself wildly in Winnie's curls, to the great consternation of the dogs. But Cyril might do anything with him, and could never do wrong. In this, Mark Antony differed from his mistress, since Cyril was the only person with whom she ever quarrelled, the two having had many a pitched battle in their childhood, though they always stood up for each other to such an extent that, if one was punished by the deprivation of pudding, the other was permitted to go on half rations with the delinquent, and to give one an orange meant to give each half a one.

" Did you tell him that the Everards were here this afternoon ? " Mrs. Maitland added, the personal pronoun being considered sufficient indication to Lilian of her brother, while " her " in addressing Cyril was known to mean Lilian.

"Were they, indeed? and I away, of course," grumbled Cyril.

"You may guess Marion's message," laughed Lilian, in a low aside, at which Cyril looked pleased.

"Well, mother, and the news?" he added.

"Henry's long silence is satisfactorily explained."

"Satisfactorily? Oh, mother! and he has been at death's door!" interrupted Lilian.

"Ill? Everard? I knew there must be something very serious," ejaculated Cyril. "But he is better?"

"He is convalescent, dear. He is a noble, unselfish fellow, as I always knew when he was but a tiny boy! He would not let his friends be written to until he was completely out of danger. There was a child dangerously ill of scarlet fever in some dreadful court in Seven Dials. He was too ill to be moved, and had a bad, drunken mother, and Henry watched him for several nights, relieving guard with a day nurse. By the time the child was out of danger Henry was raving——"

" Then, why," interrupted Cyril, with agitation, " were we not told ? "

" He had foreseen his delirium, and forbidden any communication till he died or recovered. He knew full well that nothing would have kept Marion from him, had she known—— "

" He was right ! " broke in Cyril, in a low, fervid tone. " Thank Heaven that he thought of that ! "

" Henry always thinks of everything that may affect the welfare of his friends," added Lilian, whose face wore a look of quiet enthusiasm, and whose dark grey eyes were shining with repressed tears.

" And now ? " added Cyril, with energy. " They will not let Marion go to him now, I hope. The convalescent stage is the most infectious."

" They will not meet until Henry is perfectly free from infection. You may trust Henry for that, Cyril."

" He has been very ill," said Lilian ; " they feared he would be both blind and deaf. It will be months before he can recover, though the infectious stage is already nearly past."

" Poor old Everard! that will be a terrible trial for him, with his ambition. Time is so precious to a man who is beginning his career."

" I suspect he has been working too hard," said Mrs. Maitland, " and the enforced rest to his brain may benefit him more than they think. Admiral Everard is ordered to the Mediterranean with the squadron in a few weeks' time, and, a winter abroad being necessary for Henry, he is to go in the *Cressy* to Malta, from whence he will afterwards go to other places—Egypt and the Holy Land among them—and Marion is to be his companion."

"Marion? What! Marion spend the winter abroad? Impossible! She shall not go."

" You are not married yet, Cyril," said Lilian, laughing.

" My dear boy, why should Marion not go?" asked his mother, in surprise. " She is delighted at the prospect. It is perhaps

the only chance she will have of going
abroad for any length of time. Once married,
a girl cannot see much of the world, as the
admiral says, and a country curate's wife is
especially bound to home."

"And do you suppose, mother, that I shall
always be a country curate?" asked Cyril,
with fire. "No, indeed. My wife will have
as many opportunities of seeing the world
as any one, I trust. But she cannot, she
must not leave me all this winter. I simply
cannot spare her."

"And Henry—can he spare her?" asked
Lilian.

"She is not engaged to Henry. Let
Henry get a wife of his own."

"My dear Cyril, how absurdly you talk!"
said Mrs. Maitland. "You forget that Henry
is an invalid, and will need his sister's care.
And you forget, too, that Marion is looking
forward with the greatest delight to this unexpected trip."

"The only lady on board—on board a
man-of-war!"

"And awful fun, too," interposed the boy on the rug. "I only wish I was ill, and the admiral would take me."

"Well, Lennie, you would be a more appropriate passenger, certainly. The admiral had better take us all, I think. Snip, the terrier, and Snap, the pug, with Mark Antony to catch the mice and keep us in order."

"But Marion is not going in the *Cressy*," interposed Lilian. "There was some idea of her going at first. It seems, however, that ladies are not supposed to sail with their relations."

"I was beginning to wonder whether the admiral purposed carrying a regular Noah's ark about with him," grumbled Cyril. "And pray, how does Marion get to Malta, unless in the *Cressy?* By balloon? or does she charter a vessel of her own?"

"She goes with the Wilmots, overland by Marseilles. Captain Wilmot is joining his regiment at Malta. They stop at Paris and other places, taking it leisurely, and that will be delightful to Marion, who has travelled so little."

" It seems, then, after all, that Henry will have to do without Marion till he reaches Malta," said Cyril.

" But he will have his father, and, of course, a proper attendant on board. At Malta he will be thrown on his own resources, and will need a companion. They will take care of each other," Mrs. Maitland replied cheerfully. " They think of coming home by way of Sicily."

" I shall go to Woodlands to-morrow, and remonstrate with the admiral, if he is there. I shall take the pony-chaise, unless you want it, Lilian."

" Nonsense, Cyll. You may go to the Woodlands and take the pony, but you will not remonstrate with the admiral, or make yourself in any way obnoxious," said Lilian. " When you come to reflect, you will see what a charming arrangement it is for everybody. The admiral is the more delighted, as he thinks this voyage will make Henry so desperately in love with the navy that he will become a naval surgeon."

"Hang the admiral!" observed Cyril, in his softest, most plaintive voice, while a droll little smile curved his lips. "Why doesn't somebody pity me? Isn't it hard lines, Mark Antony?"

Mark Antony responded by a tiny mew. He was sitting on the writing-table between his twin favourites, the picture of feline bliss; his tail curled round his dainty white paws, his snowy breast tinted by the ruddy fire-light, his eyes lazily closing and unclosing, while he made rhythmic accompaniment to their voices in deep, long-drawn purrs, and expressed a benevolent and condescending interest in the conversation by occasional winks and movements in the direction of brother or sister, as each spoke. He had inspected and thoroughly sniffed Cyril's sermon with an air of approving criticism.

"Mark Antony was most condescending to Marion this afternoon," said Lilian; "he not only purred affably when she stroked him, but even allowed her to kiss him on the breast."

Whereupon Cyril bestowed a salute on the same spot, commending the cat's sagacity in thus recognizing Marion as one of the family. Mark Antony drew himself up with gratified pride, and returned his friend's caress by lifting his velvet paw, placing his head on one side with an arch, roguish expression in his sparkling eyes and bristled white whiskers, and chucking Cyril under the chin with the daintiest grace, to the envy and delight of the children, who worshipped this household divinity at a distance; the jealous disgust of the dogs, who were sleeping with one eye open, after the manner of their tribe, and growled faintly; and the admiration of the whole family, who knew that this delicate caress was never accorded save to the twins.

"No one seems to have thought of me in this matter," observed Cyril, stroking the delighted animal. "I shall certainly stand up for my rights. This notion of sacrificing Marion, and sending her half the world over in charge of an invalid brother, is too detestable. Her sisters should interfere; they stand in the place of a mother to her."

"Married sisters have little influence on home affairs, fortunately for Marion's freedom in the choice of a husband," Mrs. Maitland said, laughing.

"Well, it grows late," said Cyril, rising. "By the way, I did your errands at Lee's. The eggs and the pupil are to arrive to-morrow morning."

"I am so glad you remembered," replied Lilian; "I have the greatest desire to gain some influence over Alma Lee. Do you know, Cyril, she is a girl of no common character. No one in the least suspects what that girl is capable of."

"What, Lill, have you unearthed another genius?" asked Cyril, carelessly.

"Oh no; no genius. But the next time you see her, observe the way in which her eye flashes, and the mobility of her features. Poor Alma! she is so liable to fall into temptation, with her beauty and ignorance, and

passionate, undisciplined nature. There are
fine elements in her, deep feeling, strong
imagination, and capability of self-sacrifice.
How she tended that poor little step-sister of
hers! Lucy was fearfully afflicted. Her own
mother shrank from her at times; but Alma,
never. Yet she is very wayward, and so
spoilt. Her nature is powerful for evil and
good. Nothing but strong principle can keep
such a nature straight."

Cyril listened, looking thoughtfully towards
the fire, with his hand shading his eyes from
its light.

"My sister is a profound student of human
nature, mother," he observed lightly. "She
is right in saying that Miss Alma has a will
of her own. Let us hope you will succeed in
putting a curb on this unbridled nature,
Lilian. You are quite right in your analysis
of it. But I am not sure that a Bible-class is
the panacea you imagine. To move Alma
Lee, I think you must appeal to her affections."

"She is frightfully vain, poor girl!" interposed Mrs. Maitland. "If you could induce her to dress more quietly, Lilian!"

"I am not so much afraid of her vanity, mother. As Cyril says, her affections must be got at, and I want to make my Bible-class a means to that end."

"Just listen to the parish priest!" laughed Cyril; "she talks like a book. She is worth ten curates to my father. The time I have wasted, as usual; it is past seven! Good night, Lennie. Have you earned the half-crown yet? No? Lazy fellow. You will never be able to own a menagerie as you wish, unless you work harder. You may still get the half-crown if you bring me a fable of La Fontaine's, in decent Latin, remember. Winnie has fully earned hers, and here it is, brand-new. Good night, mother. Father will be home at eight, he bid me tell you. Good night, Lilian." And, having been duly taken leave of by the dogs, Cyril left the drawing-room, accompanied to the door by Lilian and Mark Antony, the latter flourishing his tail aloft with due ceremony, and remaining seated on the step at Lilian's feet, watching till the young man's form was swallowed up in the wintry gloom.

"Cyril appears anxious to be married," Mrs. Maitland observed, on Lilian's return to the drawing-room. "It is a very strong attachment, and well placed, fortunately for the dear boy. His anxiety about Marion actually made him forget Henry's peril, and the heroism which brought it upon him. Love is stronger than friendship."

"Cyril is very impulsive," replied Lilian, "and, like all impulsive people, is in a desperate hurry about everything. An early marriage is the thing to give balance to such a temperament."

"Dear child," remonstrated her mother, "I do not think he needs balance. I may be a foolish old woman," she added, smiling, "but I can see no fault in Cyril. Neither can your father. I wish he had wider scope for his fine talents. To cramp a young fellow of his splendid powers and attainments in that narrow country parish seems such a

deplorable waste of good material.   I see, too,
that the bondage chafes him."

Lilian made no reply, but looked thoughtfully at the fire, soothing some inward perturbation by stroking and restroking Mark
Antony, who sat purring with an expression
of imbecile rapture on her knee.

Cyril meanwhile made his way through
the foggy darkness of the country roads to
his rooms in the tiny village where lay his
cure, vexed and cogitating upon every possible
means of keeping Marion in England.

His dinner was ready—a simple chop, but
cooked and served in the daintiest perfection,
and accompanied by a bottle of claret of a
delicate vintage.   Some late flowers and a
dish of autumn fruit garnished his table, all
the appointments of which were elegant and
refined.   Nothing in the simple little lattice-
windowed room could offend the most
fastidious taste, though it was rather bare,
and its easiest chair would have been full of
penance to some people's limbs.   Two proof
line-engravings, after Raphael, were its sole

adornments, unless we include a great many
books, most of which were well bound, and
a harmonium. His solitary meal ended,
Cyril's landlady brought him some coffee,
made as English coffee rarely is, and served
in a lovely cup of Sèvres, the gift of Marion
Everard, and acquainted him with the fact
that an old woman had sent three times that
day, requesting him to come and read to her,
as she was taken worse.

"I'll go directly," replied Cyril. "Poor old
soul! I'm so sorry I was out when she sent;"
and he started from his seat to get his hat.
Then it struck him that he had better drink
the coffee while it was hot, and he sat down
again, and fell into a reverie, experiencing
the delicious physical languor which comes
after much air and exercise and the satisfaction of a temperate appetite, and which is so
favourable to a certain kind of mental occupation. He looked wistfully at a volume of
St. Augustine, which lay ready to his hand,
and then at his watch. "It is too late for
Martha Hale to-night," he reflected; "and,

after all, what good can I do her? Her life has been a combination of a martyr's and a saint's; she has the Bible at her fingers' ends, and caught me tripping in a quotation twice the other day. Her spiritual knowledge is such as I can only dimly guess at. I can tell her nothing that she does not know five times as well as I. Her daughter reads to her by the hour. She has no sins to confess, no doubts to calm. And it would be a sin to disturb her at this time of night." And he finished the coffee, and was soon lost in St. Augustine's " City of God," which he closed at about the time when Martha Hale's radiant soul took flight from its worn and suffering tenement. Then he slept as youth sleeps, Marion's sweet face flitting through his dreams, and her voice making melody to an accompaniment of sweetly clashing peals of the bell-music from Long's waggon team.

CHAPTER IV.

R.ATHER more than a year after Alma Lee's
evening ride in the waggon, a railway
carriage containing two travellers was speeding southwards through the wintry air, with
din and rattle and smoke, in the wake of the
red-eyed engine, which panted, groaned, and
throbbed as with the agony of some vexed
demon.

The travellers were men in the heyday
of youth, and their comfortable rugs, and
the array of books and papers with which
they were surrounded in the well-padded
carriage, marked them as among those
fortunate sons of earth who are absolved
from the labour of carefully considering
sixpences and shillings before converting
them into things of convenience or pleasure.

An odour as of a recently evanished cigar of
fine flavour further emphasized their emanci-
pation from the slavery of petty economies,
though a practised observer would never for
a moment have classed them in the ranks of
those gilded youth who are exempted from
the curse of labour and at liberty to squander
the rich prime of their strength on pleasures
and follies as they will. No; they were
evidently two young men of the cultured
middle class, bred in comfort, if not luxury,
but with their own standing yet to make—a
truly happy position for youth of average
thews and sinews.

They sat in opposite corners, with their
legs stretched out beneath their warm rugs,
one looking backwards at the swiftly receding
perspective of trees and fields, villages and
farmsteads, flashing and fading on the sight;
the other facing forwards to the yet unseen,
but seeing it not, since he was fast asleep.
Fast asleep, unconscious and peaceful as any
babe on its mother's breast, he was speeding
on without fear to a fate which in his wildest

dreams he could never have pictured, and which, could it have been shadowed forth ever so dimly to him, he would have dismissed with laughing scorn as utterly improbable— nay, impossible. Yet the train rushed on with pant and puff and clatter, bearing him nearer and nearer to the hidden terror with every quiet breath he drew in his secure slumbers, while pleasant fancies of the present and warm hopes of the future wove themselves into fantastic images in his light dreams. His was a well-built, manly form, and his sleeping face, with all its placid calm, was full of latent energy and bright intellect; a strong, serene face, with firm lips and chin, the face of a man who could do and endure much; a face expressive of healthy vigour of both mind and body, though it bore traces of fatigue, which the soft touches of sleep were every moment erasing.

His wakeful companion was a clergyman, a man whose mobile and finely cut features, and eyes full of intense blue light, were expressive of something akin to genius; a man whose delicately organized nature could be touched, the observer would imagine, only to the finest issues.

A world of thought and care sat on the young priest's brow, and the look which he bent on the fast-receding fields was so profoundly sad, that it would seem as if happiness could never again smile on him. None of the layman's calm strength and wholesome serenity was his; such power as his face expressed would come in lightning flashes of brief but keen intensity. All nerve, fire, imagination, and feeling, was this young spirit apparently; capable of descending to the lowest depths of suffering or rising to the very airiest summits of enthusiasm. It was an eminently beautiful and spiritual young face, and one which never failed to awaken interest, if not love. He looked very worn and fatigued; but no merciful wing of sleep came to fan the trouble from his brow, while his companion slept so serenely and dreamed so pleasantly.

In one hand he held a little book with

red edges; but, instead of consulting its pages, his eyes were bent fixedly on the flying wintry landscape, which, nevertheless, they saw not, their gaze of intense abstraction being turned inwards upon some unspeakable sorrow. His face was in the shadow, while some rays of wintry sunlight fell upon the sleeper's face, touched the brown moustache with tints of gold, and finally dazzled the closed eyes to wakefulness. They were very pleasant eyes when opened—honest, hazel eyes, looking directly and kindly upon the world, and suggesting the sunshine of wholesome mirth in their depths; shrewd eyes, for they had seen many varieties of human beings in the course of six and twenty years, and were not easily deceived.

"Upon my word," observed the owner of the eyes, "I think I must have forgotten myself for a moment, Cyril."

At the first sound of his voice all the sadness vanished from the young priest's face; the mournfully brooding eyes left the landscape, and flashed a gay brilliance upon the face in the sunshine; the finely moulded lips lost their drooping curve in a smile; the dejected attitude became one of alert repose; the whole man was changed.

"You may have forgotten yourself, old fellow, but it was impossible for any one else to forget you with that dulcet harmony of yours resounding through the brain," he replied.

"Come, now, that's a libel; I never snore," returned the other, with a hearty yawn that brought the tears into his eyes; "and if I did, you might forgive me, since you were not preaching."

"There are some sermons of mine just over your head, Everard; who knows but some lulling influence may have emanated from them?"

"'He jests at scars that never felt a wound.' You scoundrel, you know very well that the sleep of the just is murdered the moment you begin thumping the pulpit-cushion," said Everard, with a banter which veiled an honest enthusiasm for his friend's gifts.

" I suppose I ought to say something neat
with regard to the elegance with which
you take off people's legs and tie up their
arteries. But, you see, my ignorance is so
total—— "

" Exactly. Genius in our profession is
known only to the initiated, while in yours
it is impossible to hide its light under a
bushel. Lucky fellows, you parsons. Not
the minutest spark of worth in you escapes
observation."

" You have hit on the weak point in our
profession, Henry," said Cyril, dropping his
air of banter. " Seriously, it is a very awful
thing to be placed as we are in the full light
of public observation, all our weaknesses,
failings, and errors heightened by its glare,
and doing—oh, the smallest of them!—such
worlds and worlds of harm."

" Stuff, Maitland! That is where you
parsons err. You think too much of your
example and influence. You don't suppose,
man, that we think you superior to human
weaknesses? Not a bit of it; we should

loathe you, if we did. For goodness sake, Cyril, don't take up with these superfine priestly notions. By the way, why didn't you go to sleep? You look as if you wanted it badly enough. Have you got some infernal machine secreted under your waistcoat, to wake you with a timely dig in case you succumb to nature's weakness, according to the rule of St. What's-his-name?"

"My dear fellow," returned the other, with a pained look, "you mean no harm, but you handle certain subjects with a levity——"

"Come now, Cyril, we are not treading on holy ground. Your conscience and feelings are in a state of hyper-æsthesia; you have been working too hard. I didn't mean that parsons were not expected to practise what they preach a little more precisely than other men, or that any grave lapse on their part is not worse in them than in others. But I object to this morbid self-consciousness and conscience-searching. Surely a clergyman who is honest in his faith ought to be able to lead a Christian's life with sufficient ease to prevent him from torturing himself about the effect of his peccadilloes, which are all taken for granted, on his flock."

" There are no peccadilloes for us," returned Cyril, with a deep sigh. "But now, Henry, let me speak out my anxiety about you as a friend merely, not as a priest. Many things you have said lately have grieved me. deeply——"

" Oh, I know! Because I don't believe in the devil, I am in a parlous state. You priests have a great tenderness for that absurd old devil of yours. Beg his pardon; I will speak more respectfully of him in future. Drive on."

" Your profession," pursued Maitland, with a look of shocked forbearance, " is a noble one; nay, in some respects it is more noble than the priesthood itself, though lacking the special stamp of sanctity which that bears. It is more noble because it involves so much more self-sacrifice. But it is one beset with special and awful dangers. Your minds are so constantly set upon the material, that it is no wonder if you are tempted to lose sight of the spiritual."

" That I admit," returned Everard.

" You risk your souls that you may heal our bodies, and the Italian proverb, ' Where there are three doctors there are two atheists,' is daily verified."

" Granted. But I am not one of the atheists, happily for me."

" Not yet; but I tremble for you, Henry. That light tone grows upon you. And you reason every day more and more from the point of view of the man of science, You learn more and more to distrust everything that cannot be proved by the evidence of the senses——— "

" Of reason."

" It amounts to the same thing. Will you promise to pray against this, Henry ? " asked Cyril, with intense supplication.

" My friend," returned the other, with a slight shake of his body, like that a dog gives in issuing from the water, " you accused me just now of treating sacred things with levity.

Now your words jar upon my sense of reverence, which is strangely different in a priest
and a layman. You are accustomed, you see,
to handle religious topics freely. I am not.
And as I have no words to express them in,
I would rather leave them alone."

Cyril heaved a profound sigh, and was
silent for some seconds, while Everard kindled
a second cigar.

"You think I have taken a liberty, Harry?"
he asked, after a while.

" Not in the least. Feeling as you do, you
would have been wrong to be silent. You
have but done your duty, old friend. Cheer
up. Oh, do keep a fellow company in a
cigar! It is holiday-time."

Cyril's sensitive face brightened. It was
evident that he was extremely anxious about
the effect his words would have on his friend's
estimation of him. But he resolutely declined
the cigar—a self-denial which fretted his
friend as being quite a new feature in his
character.

"You are very much changed, Maitland,

during the past year," he said, looking keenly at him.

"I am indeed," he replied, with a heavy sigh; and he turned the subject by pointing out the towers of a grey cathedral in the distance. "It is always a pleasant friend to meet on one's way home," he said; and the two joined in admiring the massive pile, till their passage through a chalk cutting hid it from their sight for a time, and then the train slackened, the shouts of porters were heard, the cathedral appeared once more, and they glided under the roofs of the smoky station, amid a confused din of bell-ringing, door-banging, hurrying steps and wheels, and all the turmoil attending a brief pause on a main line.

"Belminster always had a great fascination for me," observed the doctor, looking across the sea of smoke-wreathed roofs to the vast towers of the cathedral. "Surely that serenely majestic person in gaiters is the bishop himself. The expression 'Church dignitary' is so fit. Who ever heard of a medical dignitary,

or a legal dignitary? Good gracious me,
Maitland, what an awful thing it must be to
be a bishop's son! Fancy asking that urbane
and dignified cleric to pass the wine! I
should faint if called upon to feel a spiritual
lordship's pulse.

Cyril smiled as the unconscious bishop
made a stately and solitary progress past their
carriage, recognizing the young clergyman
as he passed.

"He is very kind and fatherly," he observed,
as the train moved on. "I wish I were still
in his diocese. Yes, I have a great regard
for Belminster. I was ordained there."

"May you walk in the gaiters of that good
old gentleman, Cyril, some score of years
hence, and make the splendid old arches of
the minster ring with your eloquence! I shall
settle near you—as parish doctor, mind—
though I invent heaven knows how many
diseases, as I hope to do, and Europe rings
with my discoveries. No fashionable physician
business for me."

"A bishop," observed the young priest,

thoughtfully, "has an immense scope for action."

"Here is a man," said Everard, appealing to the windows and sides of the carriage, "who is too honest to say, 'Nolo episcopari.' Let us make much of this man! Let us— hem!—marry him to our sister."

"This day two months," added Maitland, "the wedding will take place."

"By the way, the young minx suggested that I should read Tennyson's 'St. Simeon Stylites' at the next Penny Readings. The suggestion is, I suppose, intended for a profound joke. Rather a weak poem. Lunacy requires the master-mind of a Shakespeare to handle it without repulsiveness."

"I am not sure that it *was* lunacy," said Cyril.

"Not lunacy to stand on a pillar for thirty years? My good fellow, when I consider the doings of the Stylites and the recluses of the Thebaïd, I sometimes wonder if there was any sanity in the world in those days."

"There was, at least, method in their mad-ness, Everard. Consider the power their austerities gained them over the minds of ordinary men."

" Of course ; many an authentic maniac has been honoured with almost divine honours in certain stages of society. The lust of power is a curious thing. For my part, I would rather be a nonentity than stand on a pillar to gain influence."

" But consider what they wanted influence for. To bring souls to God."

" So they persuaded themselves, no doubt. Of all things I loathe asceticism. Not so much for the spiritual ambition and pride that attend it, as because it is in reality only the other side of profligacy, or, in other words, an ascetic is a rake turned monk."

" Can a rake do better than turn monk ? "

" In my judgment, he can. He can repent, turn away from his wickedness, and lead a rational human life."

" Nay. He has made himself unworthy of those common human enjoyments in which innocent men may indulge. Nothing but a life of penance can atone—— "

" Nothing can atone," interrupted Everard. " I am a Protestant, Cyril—a rabid Protestant, as you observed the other day. None of your popish penances for me. What's the matter ? "

" Nothing," replied Cyril, whose features quivered with pain, as he pressed his hand to his side. " At least, only a 'stitch' I am subject to. Myself, I long for more austerity in the Christian life of to-day. A few eremites of the Thebaïd type on Salisbury Plain—— "

" I tell you what, Cyril : you must learn to moderate your transports in that parish of yours, or you will soon be in a hospital or a lunatic asylum. Subject to a stitch at four and twenty ! It won't do. The devil fly away with your eremites ! There are legends of some of those same Thebaïd lunatics, who, after passing years and years in every species of austerity, suddenly burst their unnatural trammels in one unguarded moment, fled to

the city, and plunged into a very vortex of
iniquity. Extremes meet, and Nature is a
stern avenger."

The spasm again flitted across Cyril's face,
unnoticed by his friend, for Cyril turned to
the window as he pressed his side. Beneath
his clothes he wore a little golden cross,
studded with tiny spikes, which, on pressure,
pierced the flesh.

"The exception rather proves the rule,"
he said, smiling, as he turned his face again
towards his friend. "The ascetics have in
all ages of the world been the salt of the
earth. A mere protest against sensuality is
something. And people need the discipline
of pain."

"If I were to invent a purgatory, Cyril, it
would be one of happiness. Joy is the true
educator and refiner, not pain. Nothing
exists, or can exist, without joy, which is
both the originator and sustainer of life in
the organic world, and therefore, by analogy,
in the spiritual. You and I are here to-day
as the result of long ages of physical and

moral well-being enjoyed through an infinite chain of ancestors. Without continued physical, mental, and moral enjoyment throughout our own individual lives, you and I would never have attained to our present physical, mental, and moral stature—such as it is. Good heavens, Cyril! think of the stunted, stifled natures we have been seeing daily in those dens of East-End vice and misery, and contrast them with the men who were our companions at Cambridge!"

"I grant a certain necessary basis of physical well-being," rejoined Cyril, wearily; "but I trust the day will dawn when you too will rejoice in the discipline of sorrow. It may even now be knocking at your doors; for you are too happy, Harry, for a sinful man——"

"I am most perfectly happy, and trust to remain so, my gruesome prophet," said Everard, with a cheery laugh. "I have youth, health, a clear conscience, a profession I love, and good prospects in it, and— and——" Here a curious smile, and some-

thing distantly resembling a blush, irradiated
the doctor's face. " In short, I should be an
ungrateful miscreant if I were not perfectly
happy. Though, to be sure," he added, " I
am not going to be married to one of the
dearest girls on earth this day two months.
Why, what is this? Oldport already, as I
am a living man!" He was on his feet in a
moment, eagerly scanning the faces on the
platform, while Cyril collected the various
impedimenta. "She is not there," he muttered, in a tone of disappointment, as he
appropriated his own share of the plunder.

"Oh no!" returned Cyril, in a composed
manner; "she had no intention of coming.
Lilian would come alone; the phaeton only
holds three, and Marion, of course, would not
drive in alone."

Everard smiled at the different significance
of the word " she " in his own and his friend's
vocabulary: to the latter it meant Marion;
to himself, Lilian.

" Perhaps she *is* here, after all," he continued, " waiting outside with the pony."

"Go and see," said Cyril; "time and patience, meanwhile, may result in the production of a porter, which event I will abide."

Everard eagerly strode along the little platform, thronged with labourers and market-women bearing baskets of the singularly aggressive nature affected by market-women— baskets constructed apparently for the express purpose of damaging passengers' ribs, and finding out their tenderest spots. He threaded his way eagerly through these perils, occasionally removing a stolid and motionless human obstacle by the simple process of placing his hands on its shoulders and wheeling it aside, till he issued on the top of the hill outside the station. The river flowed peacefully by its wharves at the foot of the hill; the little town rose on its banks, and clustered lovingly round the base of the tall white tower, whose weathercock burned golden in the clear wintry sky; and the grey downs laid their arms protectingly round this, their child.

But Everard did not look at this scene; he

scanned only the lines of flys and omnibuses,
each manned by a gesticulating, whip-waving
driver, in search of the well-known pony from
Malbourne, with the face he loved behind
it. But there was no pony and no Lilian,
and he returned disconsolate to Cyril, who,
in the mean time, had succeeded in gaining
the attention of one of the two distracted
porters.

"Perhaps," observed Cyril, tranquilly, "I
forgot to write. Who knows? Well, we
must have a fly."

"By the sword of my grandfather," cried
Everard, "I will not go in one of those
confounded flys. Let us walk. The weather
is made for it. A country walk will drive
ascetic megrims out of your brain."

"And the portmanteaus?"

"Left till called for. We can carry our
own bags. Now, look here," he added, as
Cyril demurred, "I am not going to mortify
my flesh by riding in a cushioned fly behind
two horses, with my luggage carried for me.
I shall walk across country, bag on shoulder;

and if that is too comfortable for your reverence, you can get some dried peas at the first grocer's we come to."

Cyril laughed and consented. Everard gave the man silver to buy peas to put in his boots, to his great mystification, and the two young men set off down the hill, deafened by the importunities of flymen, and crossed the bridge over the dark, sluggish river, and admired the artistic pyramids of casks on the brewers' wharves, and rejoiced at hearing the familiar Hampshire drawl in the streets; for it was market-day, and many a rustic lounged, stolid, with open mouth, before the gay shop-windows decked for Christmas.

Presently a more musical sound made their ears tingle with pleasant home-thoughts—the sweet, melodious confusion of waggon-bells, clashing rhythmically along the street, and they soon recognized Long's fine team of horses, each proudly shaking the music from his crest, and responding to the guttural commands of William Grove, who strode along with an expressionless face and a sprig of mistletoe in his cap, cracking his whip, and accompanied by his satellite Jem, who bore holly in his hat. A faint gleam, distantly resembling a smile, spread over William's face at the greeting of the two young men, and he even went so far as to issue the strange monosyllable which brought his team to a standstill at their request, while the more youthful and impassioned Jem expanded into a distinct grin, and replied that his health was "middling."

" Well, and how are all the Malbourne folk? and are any of our people in Oldport to-day, Grove?"

" I ain't zeed none as I knows on," he replied, after profound consideration.

" Any of the Malbourne folk 'gone up the steps' to-day?" asked Everard, looking in the direction of the town hall, which was closed, with its clock glittering in the sunshine.

" Ah! 'tain't often we goos up steps," returned William, who knew well that the steps referred to were those conducting the malefactor before the magistrates at the town hall, and which were numerous and un-pleasant to climb with a burdened conscience. "We never knows, though," he added, in an unusual burst of moralizing, "who med be the next."

"I hope it won't be you, William," returned Everard; "if it is, it won't be for robbing those fine horses of their corn. Why, they look as fit as filberts," he added, patting the leader.

"It wun't be you neither, doctor," growled William, affectionately; "for all they zes as how you done for Jem Martin, a-cutting of him open and a-zewing of him up so many times, and pretty nigh pisened Mam Lee."

"Do they say that?" laughed Everard. "And this is fame, as Mr. Crummles observed, Cyril. Well, look here, William! you take these bags of ours, if you think the waggon can stand it, and fetch our portmanteaus from the station. Jem can run up the hill for them."

"Our luggage, William," explained Cyril,

"if it won't put you out of your way. We are going home on foot, and didn't know how on earth to get our things out till we met you."

After deep cogitation, and some assistance from the quicker intelligence of Jem, the nature of the service he was required to render at last dawned upon William Grove's intellect, which was apparently situated at a long distance from the material world, and he consented with gruff heartiness, and, waking all the five little peals of music with one motion of his whip, started off in the direction of the station.

"A happy New Year to you!" the two friends cried together at parting.

"And beware of going up the steps," added Everard. "Upon my word, Cyril, I should like to explore the recesses of that fellow's moral consciousness. He is apparently up to the level of the most advanced thinkers of the day. He evidently looks upon crime as a misfortune dependent upon quite extrinsic circumstances."

"They all do," returned Cyril. "It is the part of Christianity to convince the world of sin."

"Who shall say how far a man's will consents to his acts?" added Everard, musingly. "I hope some day to be able to give myself to the study of mental disease, and more accurately trace the connection between that and crime."

"Let us forget both this one day," said Cyril, whose spirits had undergone a wonderful change in the last half-hour, and were now gay even to boyishness.

Everard fell readily into his humour, and, chatting and laughing, the friends soon passed the streets of the little town and its miniature suburbs, and gained the pretty village of Chalkburne, the Norman tower of which showed in the sunlight fresh and unworn by its eight centuries of storm, and greeted the travellers with the music of its chiming hour as they walked through the linden-girdled churchyard, rejoicing in their youth and the live wintry air.

Cyril had the gift of conversation, which Everard somewhat lacked, and the talk was brilliant and sparkled with his ready wit and quick repartee, in which the doctor was continually worsted, greatly to his own good-humoured content. His love for Cyril and his admiration for his gifts were boundless. The two friends had passed all their school-time together, Everard riding daily to Malbourne to study with Cyril's tutor, Mr. Maitland's curate; and in those young days the hero-worship began, the elder boy, whose mental powers were slower, if more solid, admiring, protecting, and helping the bright-eyed, clever child who shared his studies and so often distanced him. They met again at Cambridge, where the senior was only one year ahead of his two-years junior, and there Everard found fresh cause to admire his brilliant and successful friend, who gathered friends and admirers innumerable about him, and won laurels, both literary and social.

And now family ties promised to unite them more closely, and Everard was glad—

far more glad than Maitland, whose affection for his friend, though warm, had not the slightest element of hero-worship, but was, on the contrary, flavoured with a good spice of condescension. With all his imagination and quick sympathy, Cyril did not see that Henry possessed those solid and patient mental gifts which readily master the facts of physical science, and, above all, had the peculiar faculty which may be called scientific imagination,—that he was, in short, one of those chosen few who make new epochs in the history of scientific research. Cyril looked upon his enthusiasm for his profession as praiseworthy, but inexplicable. It seemed to him that Henry crawled upon the earth, while he soared in the vast of heaven's blue. Such was the bond which united the two hard-working young men who walked along the chalky road that bracing afternoon at the end of December, to pass a week's well-earned holiday under the friendly roof of Malbourne Rectory.

CHAPTER V.

THE afternoon sun was shining peacefully upon the thatched roofs of Malbourne, on the dark grey spire of its tree-girdled church, and on the south-west front of Malbourne Rectory. At one of the sun-lighted windows sat Lilian Maitland, busily writing, her face directed to the prospect without, which she occasionally looked upon in her thoughtful pauses.

The lawn sloped quickly from the windows to a road which was concealed by trees, and beyond which rose the park-like grounds of Northover House in such a manner as to appear but a continuation of the Rectory grounds. Somewhere down in the hollow by the road there danced and murmured the bright little stream which gave its name to Malbourne, and which Lilian knew was sparkling gaily now in the sunshine, as it washed the drooping hart's-tongue waving from its mossy bank. Beyond the cluster of village roofs on the right spread a range of flat, windy fields to the unseen sea. Behind the Rectory, and on the left of Lilian's window, rose the bleak chalk downs, strong barriers against the wild salt winds which swept over those regions, summer and winter, from the sea.

Mark Antony, the cat, sat demurely on the table by the blotting-book, thoughtfully scanning the sunny landscape, and pretending not to see the pert little robin on the lawn, while he occasionally appealed to Lilian's sympathies by rubbing his velvet head against her cheek, or giving her a dainty little bite, which he had copied from his human friends, under the impression that it was a kiss. In a low chair, between the table and the fire, sat a very pretty, slender girl, toying with a piece of fancy work, but really intent upon trying to win

a glance or responsive purr from Mark
Antony, who regarded all her efforts with
haughty indifference, and continued to evolve
his philosophy of the visible universe unmoved.

"He is so tantalizing!" she cried, throwing away her work with a pretty pettish
gesture. "If he would only once show some
deference to me, I should not care. Puss,
puss, I say! Come to me at once, sir!"

"He thoroughly understands the secret of
his own supremacy, Marion," replied Lilian,
coming to the end of her writing, and softly
stroking the animal's snow-white breast.
"He knows as well as you do that you would
think nothing of his caresses if he lavished
them unasked."

"Selfish, hateful animal!"

"He is not selfish," replied Lilian; "he is
a profound student of human nature. He
has discovered that the deepest joy a human
being can taste is to love disinterestedly.
He therefore offers mankind this enjoyment
by permitting them to adore him at a

distance. Dogs afford a far lower enjoyment —that of being loved."

"Dogs are right," said Marion, her brown eyes softening in a wistful gaze; "the happiest thing is to be loved. I should die if people didn't love me. I almost hated Cyril when I thought, in that dreadful time last spring, that he didn't care for me."

"It is delicious to be loved," rejoined Lilian, "but to love is best. How happy Henry is in his affection for you! You are the dearest thing in the world to him, and yet I think you care little comparatively for him; you even prefer your brother Leslie, who is always too busy with sport and gaieties to write to you."

"Well, it is different," replied Marion. "Henry is so full of learning that he seems older than Leslie, who is the darling of his regiment and so full of life. And then, Henry is not engaged. I am sure he has never cared for any girl, and will die an old bachelor. Of course, he cares much more for me than I can for him. And he is so devoted to Cyril."

"I think," said Lilian, pressing her cheek against her pet's glossy fur, "that neither of you know the real worth of Henry."

"Oh, he is the best old fellow in the world, but not clever and handsome like Cyril, and without the dash of Leslie. By the way, I suppose those bad boys will be here to-night."

"No doubt they will turn up some time, unless something serious detains them, in which case they will telegraph. Cyll has promised to preach to-morrow. Are you quite sure, Marion, that he did not mention his train? He always likes me to meet him at Oldport."

"He said he would write later to name the train. I suppose he forgot."

"He does forget now, Marion, as he never used to. He is killing himself in that dreadful parish. Oh, I shall be so thankful when you are married! There will be a perfect holiday, to begin with, and then you will keep him within reasonable bounds."

Marion laughed. "He will have to take

care of me as well as the parish," she said.
" But what is this ? "

" This " proved to be merely Eliza, the
parlour-maid, who entered with her usual
unmoved countenance.

" It is only Stevens, Miss Lilian," she said.
" And could you please step down to the
forge at once ? "

" The forge ! " exclaimed Marion, with
wide eyes of astonishment.

" What is the matter there, Eliza ? " asked
Lilian, tranquilly.

" Only Hotspur, Mr. Ingram's horse, miss.
They've been trying this hour to get him
shod. Straun says he wouldn't touch him
for a hundred pounds."

" But what has the parish clerk to do with
shoeing horses ? " exclaimed the bewildered
Marion.

" Or the parson's daughter ? " added
Lilian, laughing. " Why, nothing is done
in the village without Stevens, Marion. He
and Grandfer together are the oracles of
Malbourne. No, you shall not come with

me; you would be frightened to death. Go
and see if mother wants anything. She will
be waking now."

"Oh, I say, Lilian!" cried a little voice, as
Lennie burst in, rosy and excited, " do come
along. Such larks! Hotspur has kicked a
cart to atoms, and now he is letting fly in all
directions, and is killing Judkins, and there's
Stevens stamping at the back door, and the
whole village with its hair on end."

"Hyberbole is Lennie's favourite figure,"
commented Lilian, going out into the hall,
and taking her hat and jacket. "Run on,
Lennie, and say I am just coming. Matter?
Oh, my dearest Marion, nothing! Only that
Ingram Swaynestone spoils his horses'
tempers, and then is surprised that his
servants can't manage them."

In another minute Lilian had passed with
quick, light step and erect carriage down the
drive, and along the village high-road,
bordered with its little gardens, in which
one or two belated autumn flowers still made
a brave show against the wintry rigour. She

went quickly, but without hurry, and found
time on the way to give some directions about
the church to the clerk, a lean, rugged figure,
stooping slightly beneath the fardel of some
fifty winters, and crowned with a shock of
grizzled red hair, who walked and talked
excitedly at her side.

Soon she saw the forge, from the black
heart of which streamed a ruddy glow, looking lurid in contrast with the sunshine, and
round which was grouped a dense little
crowd of women and children, with a few
men. Straun, the smith, a burly, grimy,
bare-armed figure in a leathern apron, stood
in an attitude of defiant despair, one strong
hand grasping his great hammer, which he
had flung on the anvil, and calling silently
on Heaven to witness that he was ready
to shoe Christian horses, however rampant, but
not demons, hippogriffs, or any such uncanny
monsters. Near him, looking rather pale,
but resolute, as became one superior to the
weaker emotions, an old, bent, withered man,
with shrewd grey eyes and pursed-up mouth,

stood leaning forward on a stout oaken stick,
and shook his head as one who despaired of
finding virtue in these degenerate days in
either man or beast.

" And I zays, as I ʹzed afore," he repeated,
emphasizing his words with the stick, which
he dug into the ground with all the force of
his two withered hands, " zend for Miss
Lilian—zend for she ! "

" Lard love 'ee, Granfer," observed a stout
fellow in a smock-frock, who stood inside the
forge in attendance on a couple of massive,
glossy-coated cart-horses, who were cosily
munching some hay dropped before them, and
contemplating the proceedings lazily with
their great soft winking eyes, " where's the
use of a gal ? "—a proposition received by
Granfer and the assembled village with silent
scorn.

The centre of the excited little crowd,
which occasionally burst asunder and flew
outwards with a wild mingling of women's
and children's shrieks—for the men skurried
off with a silent celerity that was all the more

effectual—was a beautiful chesnut horse, not standing, according to the comfortable and decent wont of horses, on four firmly planted feet, but outraging people's belief in the stability of natural laws by rearing himself wildly and insecurely on his two hind legs, and dangling from his mouth in mid-air a miserable white-faced biped in sleeved waistcoat and gaiters, whose cap had fallen off, and whose damp hair streamed as wildly as Hotspur's own waving mane and quivering tail. Tired of this folly, with his ears laid back, his nostrils wide and red, and his eyes showing nothing but the whites, Hotspur would suddenly drop his victim to his native earth, and, plunging forwards on his other end, as if intent on turning a summerset, would throw his hind hoofs up towards the sky in a manner most alarming to those who enjoyed a near view of the proceedings; and then, wearying of this, he would dance round on all four legs at once in a manner utterly bewildering to contemplate.

" Why, Hotspur," cried Lilian, in her clear,

mellow voice, as she stepped quickly through
the crowd just as Hotspur dropped the unfortunate groom to the ground, and prepared
to turn himself the other way up, " what is
this, old fellow ? " and she caught the rein
from the groom's hand, pushing the latter
gently away, and laid her slender, strong
white hand firmly upon the quivering neck
of the maddened, plunging horse. " Fie,
Hotspur, fie ! "

No one had observed Lilian's approach, and
when she appeared, as if dropped from the
skies in the groom's place, a sudden quiet
pervaded every human face and limb, the
crowd fell back, and all looked on, save the
sceptic with the cart-horses, with an air of
tranquil expectancy ; while Lilian, without a
trace of anxiety or agitation, talked in
caressing, reproving tones to the ill-conducted
steed, whose limbs had quivered into some
approach to quiet at the first touch of the
slender, spirit-like hand on his neck.

But even Lilian's magic touch could not
expel the demon of passion at once from the

maddened creature. He still reared and plunged and danced, in a manner that led the spectators to give him plenty of room for his evolutions; but he became gradually quieter, until he stood as Providence intended horses to stand, on all four feet at once, and only betrayed the internal workings of his outraged feelings by the quivering of his limbs and body, the workings of his ears and eyes, and the redness of his wide nostrils, while Lilian's musical voice never ceased its low monologue of soothing and reproach, and her hand never left stroking and patting his shining neck and shoulders. At Hotspur's first backward rear, indeed, her hand left him perforce, and she only avoided being hoisted in mid-air like the luckless groom by giving him a long rein and stepping quickly back out of the way of his formidable fore-feet.

This was an ugly moment, and a woman in the crowd uttered an exclamation of dismay and turned pale at the sight of the girl beneath the rearing horse, though no one else betrayed the least emotion, not even

the sceptic in the smock-frock, whose mouth
was too widely opened in astonishment to
leave room for his features to express any
other feeling; but Hotspur, finding that
Lilian did not balk him of his dance on his
hind legs, soon desisted from that uncomfortable performance, and yielded, as his betters
frequently did, gradually to the soothing
charm of her voice and touch, until he became,
figuratively speaking, clothed and in his
right mind. She found fault with Hotspur's
bit, and pointed out the undue tightness of
his girths to Judkins, whose cheeks had now
resumed their native ruddy hue; and when
these defects were remedied, she led the horse
a little way along the road and back again,
and fed him with sugar and other dainties,
till Hotspur's heart waxed so glad within him
that he consented to stand like a lamb, while
Straun, not without some misgiving in his
bluff face, and a muttered reference to his
wife and his seven children, fitted his new
shoes on to his restive feet with what speed
and dexterity he could muster.

"And I zed," observed Granfer, again striking his oaken staff emphatically on the ground, and looking round on the assembled village as if for applause, " zed I, ' Zend for Miss Lilian—zend for she ' ! "

The crowd, in the mean time, had been augmented by the arrival of two other spectators, who were unobserved in the absorbing interest evoked by Hotspur and his conqueror. One was a tall, finely built man, somewhat past middle life, on a good, well-bred bay horse, which he rode and handled with perfect horsemanship. He stopped, in the first instance, to avoid riding over the village population; and in the second, to witness the curious little drama enacted in the wintry sunshine. He was soon joined by a grey-haired clergyman, of venerable aspect and refined features, who looked on with quiet interest.

"Upon my word, Maitland," said the equestrian, addressing the latter, "this is a new revelation of your daughter's powers. I was already aware that she soothed the troubles and quieted the consciences of the whole village, but I did not know that she undertook the blacksmith's labours as well."

"My daughter," replied Mr. Maitland, tranquilly, "has received a very singular gift from the Almighty. She can subdue any animal, tame or wild, by some mysterious virtue of touch, voice, or glance—perhaps of all three. Not a very lofty gift, perhaps, Sir Lionel, but one which is often very useful in a homely way."

"But surely, Maitland, you cannot approve of Lilian's rendering such dangerous services as these. Are you not afraid for her ?"

"No; I have every confidence in her powers. And I do not like to make her nervous by suggesting danger. Perhaps one secret of her influence is her absolute fearlessness. Watch the expression of her eye. No; I like my child to render whatever service she is capable of to her fellow-creatures. Parents often err, I think, by interfering unnecessarily with their children's actions. Well, Lilian, and what was the matter ?" he asked, as the crowd, perceiving them, fell back respectfully, with curtsies and cap-touchings. Judkins, receiving his four-footed charge from Lilian's hand, prepared to mount and ride away, not without warning from Lilian, and strict injunctions to eschew whipping and other irritations, and to quiet Hotspur's nerves by a good canter on the turf.

"Only a horse with a spoilt temper, father," she replied. "How do you do, Sir Lionel ? Tell Mr. Swaynestone that I mean to scold him roundly about Hotspur. He is far too hot himself to be able to indulge in chesnut horses. And, indeed, I am not sure that he ought to have any horse at all."

"All this," said Sir Lionel, who had dismounted and taken off his hat with graceful, old-fashioned courtesy, "I will faithfully do, though surely one word from yourself would have more effect than volumes I could say. Do your spells work only on the lower creation, Lilian ?"

"I suppose so," returned Lilian, turning

homewards in the reddening sunbeams, accompanied by the two gentlemen and the horse, which latter she patted to his great satisfaction. " My spells consist chiefly of sympathy and affection, and these are perfect with innocent animals and children, but only partial with sinful men."

" Ben Lee will never forgive you for inducing me to drive without bearing-reins," said Sir Lionel. " I wish you could have seen the sight, Maitland. Lee ignominiously dethroned, your daughter and myself on the box, Lilian handling the ribbons, and driving me up and down before the house without bearing-reins. Lee never drives out now without preparing for his last moment, poor fellow. I hope you will not help poachers, Lilian. I hear you can surround yourself with fifty pheasants at any moment in our woods."

" If I were to hurt anything, I think my power would be gone ; and even if I did not love a thing I should have no power, for I have no influence on reptiles."

"And does Cyril, who is so like you, share your power?"

"As a child he did," interposed Mr. Maitland. "You remember the bull that killed Lee's father, Sir Lionel? Imagine my feelings on seeing the twins, then about six years old, stroking him, and trying to reach by jumping up to his terrific horns! Still, Cyril has an unusual influence over animals, though it becomes fainter. He has more power with human beings than his sister."

"Yet Lilian stopped that fellow who was beating his wife to death."

"And the whole village looking on and not lifting a finger—the cowards!" Lilian flashed out. "He fell down in sheer fright when I rushed at him. Come in, Sir Lionel, and have some tea," she added, as they reached the gates.

But Sir Lionel refused the tea, having still some distance to ride before dark.

"I am in Lady Swaynestone's service to-night," he said, "and she bid me ask you to come and counsel her about some distribution of coals or what not, when you have a spare moment. I wish you could also exorcise the demon of extravagance from that boy Ingram."

" She nearly scolds the poor fellow to death as it is," said Mr. Maitland. " We are expecting Henry Everard to-night."

" So I hear. A promising fellow, Sir Andrew Smithson tells me. He was both clever and kind in his treatment of Lee's wife last spring. As a lad, I thought him rather dull. However, we all pin our faith on Dr. Everard now at Swaynestone."

And bidding them farewell, Sir Lionel sprang like any youth to his saddle, and rode away at a canter, looking like a very prince, as his tall and gracefully erect figure disappeared among the trees in the dusk.

The group at the forge, meantime, rightly judged that so much heat, toil, and anxiety required the alleviation of moisture, and Straun, casting his hammer aside, proclaimed his intention of adjourning for solace to the Sun, which stood at the corner by the cross-roads, a few paces further down the road.

"Come on, Stevens," he said, "and toss me who'll treat Granfer."

The guardian of the cart-horses thought it a pity not to follow so good an example; so also did Hale, the wheelwright, who lived at the opposite corner; and Wax, who chanced to be the schoolmaster, and Baines, the tailor, whose monotonous indoor occupation, though varied with pig-jobbing and gardening, required frequent solace of this nature. Hale's brother Tom, a soldier resting from war's alarms in his native village in a very undress uniform, consisting of no belt, a tunic unbuttoned all the way down and displaying a large expanse of striped shirt, trousers tucked up round the ankles, a short pipe, and a muffin-cap perilously askew, considered it a breach of manners unbecoming a soldier and a gentleman to permit these worthy men to drink without his assistance; and similar feelings animated his brother Jim, a sailor, bearing the legend, "H.M.S.

Bellerophon," on his cap. So the brave fellows, accommodating their pace to that of Granfer, which was more dignified than swift, turned in as one man beneath the low doorway of the Sun, and grouped themselves about the cosy, sanded bar, where the firelight was beginning to look cheerily ruddy in the fading afternoon.

" And I zaid," added Granfer, striking the sanded floor dogmatically with his stick, " ' Zend for Miss Lilian—zend fur she.' "

" Ay, Granfer," growled the smith, " it's all very well for Miss Lilian. She ain't got a wife and seven children, and her bread to git."

" I zes, zes I," interposed the sceptic in the smock-frock, who had taken a pull at his tankard, and was removing the foam from his lips by the simple application of the back of his hand, " ' Where's the use of a gal ? ' I've a zin it, and I believes it. I shouldn't a believed it if I hadn't a zin it."

" You never believes nothink," observed Jim. " Ah! if you'd a sin what I've a sin aboord the *Bellyruffian*—— "

"Or if he'd a sin they there snake-charmers in India, what he won't believe in," added the soldier.

"Ah!" broke in the clerk, "you put Miss Lilian aboord the *Bellyruffian*, or take her out to Injy and let her charm snakes, and I'll war'nt she'll do it. That ar buoy Dick, whatever she done to he, nobody knows. A bad 'un he wer, wouldn't do nothing he hadn't a mind to. You med bate 'un till you couldn't stand. Wax have broke sticks about his back, and covered 'un with weals, but catch he gwine to school if he'd a mind to miche. I ses to Miss Lilian, I ses, 'I've a bate that ar buoy black and blue,' I ses, 'and I've a kep 'un without vittles this two days, and he wun't do nothun he an't a mind to.' And she ups and ses, 'Stevens,' she ses, 'I should like to bate you,' she ses; 'I should like to bate you green and yaller,' she ses. 'Lard love 'ee, Miss Lilian, whatever would ye bate I for?' I ses, ses I. 'Because you are a fool, Stevens,' she ses, 'and you are ruining that buoy, and turning

him into a animal,' she ses. And she took
'un up Rectory, and kep' 'un there a day, and
sent 'un home as good as gold. And she
made me promise I wouldn't bate 'un no more
for two good weeks, and I ain't bate 'un
zince, and he'll do what he's told now
without the stick. 'I should like to bate
you green and yaller, Stevens,' she ses. And
she'd a done it, she would, green and yaller
—ah! that she would, mates."

"I don't deny," said Baines, the tailor,
whose profession rendered him morbid, revolu-
tionary, and inclined to distrust the utility
of existing institutions, "but what Miss
Lilian may have her uses."

"Ah, Baines," interrupted the soldier,
" you ain't such a fool as you looks, after all."

Before the stupefied Baines, who was
accustomed to have his remarks received
with reverence, could reply to this insult,
public feeling was suddenly outraged by the
following observation from the smock-frocked
sceptic, the want of wisdom in whom was
accounted for by his having only recently

come to Malbourne from a village at least
ten miles off that centre of intelligence.

"But what shall us do when Miss Lilian
gets married ? "

"Married ! " shouted the clerk. " And
who ses she's a-gwine to marry ? "

"She med marry ; then agen she medn't,"
replied this foolish person, unabashed by the
dark glances bent upon him.

" Miss Lilian," observed Granfer, who had
been indulgently listening while he despatched
his beer, and thus affording weaker wits the
opportunity of exercising themselves during
his forbearance, "ain't agwine to marry
nobody ; " and, thrusting his staff forwards
and resting his two hands upon it, Granfer
looked round the assembly with austere
menace in his shrewd grey eyes.

Nobody dared reply to this, and silence
prevailed, broken only by the sound of good
liquor disappearing down men's throats, and
a weak, half-audible murmur from the smock-
frock about girls being girls, whether gentle
or simple.

" I zes to my missus, vive year agone last
Middlemas, zes I," continued Granfer, who
chanced to be the grandsire of the indignant
clerk, " ' Miss Lilian ain't one o' your
marrying zart ; ' " and again Granfer looked
round the assembly as if challenging them
to deny the undeniable, and was met by an
assenting murmur of " Ah's ! "

" Miss Lilian," pursued Granfer, with an
air of inspiration, " is turned vour and
twenty. Vour and twenty year old come
last May is they twins. Well I minds the
night they was barned. The last time as
ever I druv a 'oss. A vrosty night 'twas,
and nipped all the archards miles round, and
there warn't no vruit that year. Ah!
Varmer Long he'd a lost dree and dirty
yowes lambing-time that year. Well I minds
it. I druv pony-chaise into Oldport, and
vetched out t' doctor. And I zes to my missus,
I zes, when I come home, ' Master's got twins ! '
Ay, that's what I zed, zure enough. And
my missus she zes, zes she, ' Lard love 'ee,
Granfer,' she zes, ' you don't zay zo ! ' she

zes ; " and again Granfer paused and looked
round to perceive the effect of his eloquence.

"Ay," said the landlord, feeling that
courtesy now obliged him to entertain the
intellects as well as the bodies of his guests,
"twins is zummat when it comes to that.
Twins is bad enough for poor volk, but when
it comes to ladies and they, Lard 'a massey ! "

"Ah ! " murmured Granfer, shaking his
head with profound wisdom, and at the same
time regretfully contemplating the vacuum
in his beer-pot, " them twins done for Mrs.
Maitland. She ain't ben the zame 'ooman
zince, never zimmed to perk up agen arter
that. Vine children they was, too, as ever
you'd wish to zee, and brought up on Varmer
Long's Alderney cow, kep' special vor 'um,
as I used to vetch the milk marnin' and
evenin'. I did, zure enough."

Here Tom, the soldier, who, in virtue of
his red coat, was bound to be susceptible to
feminine charms, opined that Miss Lilian was
still "a smartish-looking gal ; " and Jim, the
sailor, added that he didn't see why she

shouldn't pick up some smart lad yet, for his heart was warm, and he could not bear to consign an unoffending girl to the chills of single blessedness. There was Lieutenant Everard, of the *Bellerophon*, a frequent visitor at the Rectory, for example—as smart an officer as Jim had ever seen, he added.

" Ah, goo on wi' ye ! " cried Granfer, greatly refreshed by the polite replenishment of his pot at Tom's expense. " Miss Lilian's as pretty a maid as Tom'll zee in a day's march. But she wun't marry nobody. Vur why ? zes I. Cause she wun't ha'e the common zart, and the upper crust they wun't ha'e she."

" W'atever's come over Judkins now ? " asked Hale, the wheelwright, musingly. " He'd had a drop too much 's afternoon, and he was a latherin' into Hotspur like mad coming down shoot.* He hadn't ought to treat a hoss like that."

" A man med well drink," said the tailor, " afore trusting hisself to a animal like that

* A short steep hill on the highway.

there.   Steady as Charlie Judkins was, poor chap!   What these 'ere rich men 'a got to answer for ! "

" I never zeen a 'oss rampageouser," replied the smith ; " but I never zeen a 'oss Miss Lilian couldn't quiet, or a ass either."

" Your missus 'ull be sending for her one day, then," said Jim ; and the whole assembly broke into a loud guffaw, after which Granfer very impressively related the history of the hunted fox, which appeared one day with his paws on the window-sill of Lilian's sitting-room, followed by the pack in full cry, and the whole field at no great distance. He told how Lilian quickly opened the window, Reynard leapt in, and she as quickly shut it; and how the huntsman, on finding the hounds at check round the Rectory window, looked in, and was greatly shocked to see poor Reynard's pointed nose and glittering eyes peering out from among the skirts of a young lady sitting quietly at work, and tranquilly surveying the baffled hounds baying outside.

Lilian refused to deliver up her fugitive, holding parley with the master of the hounds through the closed and latched window, until the latter had withdrawn his pack; and it was not until the premises had been cleared a good half-hour of every vestige of hound, horse, and man, that she unbolted door or window, and suffered her weary, panting prisoner to depart, which he did with evident regret and thankfulness for hospitality—a hospitality poorly requited by him, since he managed to snatch a chick from the poultry-yard in effecting his escape.

But no one seemed to think there was anything unusual in Lilian's power over living creatures; it was simply what one expected of Miss Lilian, just as one expected church bells to ring and cocks to crow. Nor had any one thanked her for assisting so effectively at the shoeing of Hotspur.

Then followed a long history of animals healed by Lilian, and in particular of a dog of Ingram Swaynestone's, which the latter was going to shoot, when she begged its life,

and nursed it into health. Also of the
racers Ingram had at a trainer's, and the
money he lost by them; of the oaks and
beeches at Swaynestone, which had to expiate
these losses; and of the young fellow's pro-
bable descent to beggary through the paths
of pleasure.

"He's a vine young veller," observed
Granfer, at the close of his second pot; "a
wild 'un zurely. His vather was a wild 'un,
too; 'tis the blood and the high veeding. So
was his grandfather. I minds things as Sir
Lionel did would make 'ee all stare. Men is
just the zame as 'osses—veed 'em up, and they
vlings. The well-bred 'uns is vive times
skittisher than t'others. Wuld Sir Lionel, he
was the wildest of all—druv his stags into
Oldport vour-in-hand, he did, and killed dree
or vour volks in the streets. Ah! times isn't
what they was," sighed Granfer, regretfully
draining his pot.

By this time it was dark night. The Sun
windows threw a warm glow over the road;
the stars sparkled keenly above the thatched

roof of the little hostel; and the smell of
wood-smoke, mingled with the appetizing
odour of fried pork, red herrings, and onion
soup, rising all over the village, warned the
topers that the hour of supper was approaching, and they would have dispersed,
however unwillingly, but for the chimes of
waggon-bells along the road, which beguiled
them into waiting while William Grove
deposited his parcels at the Sun, took the one
glass offered by the host, and recounted the
news from Oldport.

CHAPTER VI.

ON looking back in after-life to that brisk winter's walk, both Everard and Maitland held it as one of their sunniest memories. Every step seemed to put a fresh lustre in Cyril's eyes, and add to the wine-like sparkle of his conversation. In proportion as his spirits fell at one time, they rose at another by virtue of his sensitive, emotional temperament; while Henry's steady, sunny cheerfulness went on deepening more slowly, but perhaps more surely, and at last bubbled over. Presently they passed a woman toiling up a hill with a baby and a basket, of both which burdens Everard relieved her, to her unbounded surprise, coolly handing the basket to Cyril, and himself bearing the baby, which he tossed till it crowed with ecstasy. Having left these trifles at a roadside cottage, with a shilling to requite the woman for the loan of her infant, they reached Swaynestone Park, and met Ben Lee, who was crossing the road on his way from his cottage to the stables.

Everard greeted him with a cordiality to which Lee replied gruffly, and with an evident intention of hurrying on.

"Oh, come, Lee," said Everard, "you are not so busy as all that! How are they all up at the Temple? Alma's roses in full bloom, I hope? And my patient, Mrs. Lee, has she quite got over the accident? I shall be looking in very soon."

"You may save yourself the trouble, Dr. Everard," returned Lee, in a surly manner; "thank 'ee kindly all the same. But I want no more gentlefolk up at my house. I've had enough of they. Good afternoon, Mr. Cyril; glad to see you home, sir;" and, touching his hat, he passed quickly on, leaving Everard in a state of stupefaction in the middle of the road.

"What the deuce is the matter with Lee?" he exclaimed. "Surely he can't be drunk, Cyril!"

All the light had faded from Cyril's radiant face. The moment he caught sight of the coachman, he made the old movement of pressing his hand to his side in a spasm of pain, and he seemed almost as impatient of delay as Lee himself.

"I never heard of his drinking," he replied evasively. "Perhaps things have gone wrong with him. Look here, Henry! let us cut the high-road, and get home across country; we shall save half a mile, and find the ladies at tea."

"What sense can you get out of a fellow in love?" returned Everard, leading the way over the stile. "For him mankind dwindles down to a slim puss of a girl, with dimples and a pair of brown eyes. Go on, man! 'Gather ye rosebuds while ye may;'" and, lilting out the gay old ballad with all the strength of his honest lungs, Everard resumed his light-hearted manner, and did not observe that Cyril's gaiety had become forced and spasmodic.

A ruddy glow above the wooded crests of Northover was all that remained of day when they entered the Rectory grounds by the churchyard path, and found Lilian, with the cat gravely coiled at her feet at the hall door, darkly outlined against the faint, crimson light of the hall stove.

"Your instinct is infallible, Lilian," said Cyril, embracing her; "for you were not even sure that I was coming to-night. Dear Lilian, it *is* nice to see you again!"

"I am glad not to be wholly eclipsed by the new star," she replied, laughing, yet scanning his face with some anxiety, while she continued to hold his hand. Then she turned to Henry, over whose spirits an unaccountable damp had descended, and offered him her hand; while Cyril stooped to stroke Mark Antony, who was triumphantly rubbing himself round and round his legs with loud purrs and exultant tail. "I am so glad you have brought him, Henry," she said; adding, in a lower voice, "He is looking horribly ill."

By this time Mr. Maitland, the children, the dogs, and all the servants were in the hall, greeting Cyril with such enthusiasm that Henry remained for some moments unnoticed by Lilian's side.

" You all seem extremely glad to see *Cyril*," he observed to her, with rueful emphasis.

" Dear Henry, I know we are horribly rude to our guests when we have Cyril to spoil," she replied, laying her hand gently on his arm.

He took the hand in his and pressed it warmly to his side, and felt that the rainbow radiance had suddenly returned to his universe. But the bright moment was very brief, for it was now his turn to be welcomed, and by the time he was free to go into the drawing-room, Lilian was not to be seen."

" But where is Marion ? " asked Cyril, looking round the drawing-room, after he had duly saluted his mother, who was, as usual, on her couch.

"I think you will find her in my room," replied Lilian, as indifferently as if she had not specially arranged for the lovers to meet there. "We dine punctually at half-past seven. No, Henry, you foolish fellow, you are to stay here," she added, as Cyril left the room, and Henry attempted to follow him.

"A brother, I suppose, is of no account in these days," grumbled Everard, seating himself by Mrs. Maitland's couch with a contented air, nevertheless. "All this courtship is sickening to me, Mrs. Maitland. As for that hopeful son of yours, not one word of sense have I got out of him this day, or do I expect to get for the next two months. Thank goodness, it must come to an end then, and they will settle down to a life's squabbling like sane people."

"Ah, young people! young people!" said Mr. Maitland, looking very happy about it. "We must not be hard upon them, Henry. We all go mad once—Lennie will turn that back into Latin for you, eh?—But we con-

sider Cyril and Marion a very sensible young
couple, don't we, Nellie?"

"I think," replied Mrs. Maitland, laughing,
"that we consider everything that Cyril does
sensible. When his biography is written, it
will be said that his family did, to a certain
extent, appreciate him."

Whereupon the conversation turned upon
Cyril and his doings and his prospects, and
their anxiety about him, and suddenly the
thought struck chill to Everard's marrow—
What would happen, in case of Cyril's failure,
death, or other misadventure, to the innocent
family circle of which he was the central
hope?

The curtains were drawn snugly against
the frosty cold without. Eliza, all smiles
and fresh cap-ribbons, brought a lamp and
tea; and Everard wondered if heaven could
possibly be an improvement on the present.
No one ever made or poured out tea like
Lilian, he thought; no tea ever had so divine
an effect on the nervous system as hers. For
weeks he had dreamed of sitting thus by the

drawing-room fire, his whole being pervaded
by the delicious fact of her presence, and
now he found the reality sweeter than the
dream.

Not for weeks only, but for years afterwards, did the memory of that fireside scene
shine warmly on the darkness of his life.
The lamplight was so soft that the fire, on
which Lennie had thrown some fir-cones,
disputed for mastery with it, and added to
the cheery radiance of the pretty drawing-
room.   On one side of the fire, Mrs. Maitland,
still beautiful, though faded, and exquisitely
dressed, lay on her couch amidst becomingly
arranged furs and shawls; Henry sat by her
on a low seat, and rendered her various
little filial attentions; Mr. Maitland sat facing
the fire, with its light playing on his silvery
hair and clean-cut features, the prototype
of Cyril's.

On the other side of the hearth sat Lilian,
with the tea-table at her side; Winnie was
on a stool at her feet, her head pressed to
her sister's knee, on which reposed, in care-

less majesty, Mark Antony, gracefully toying
with the golden curls tossed in pretty negli-
gence within reach of his paws. The warm
rug before the fire was occupied by the terrier
and the pug, the children's tea-cups, and the
recumbent full-length of Lennie, who sprang
to his feet from time to time to pass people's
cups.

Lilian spoke little. She and Henry did
not address each other once; but his eye
never lost the picture on the opposite side
of the fire, which reminded him of Raphael's
Virgin of the Cardellino. It was not that
Lilian's intelligent face in the least resembled
that harmless, faultlessly featured Madonna's,
though her deep grey eyes were bent down
much in the same way on the child-face and
sportive animal on her knee as the Virgin's
in the picture. It was the look of divine,
innocent, ineffable content that she wore.
And yet Everard did not appear to be looking
at this charming picture, though Lilian knew
that he saw it, and was equally conscious of
the picture he made, his broad shoulders and

athletic limbs affording a fine contrast to her mother's fragile, faded grace.

"And what are your plans, Henry?" asked Mr. Maitland at last, when Cyril's affairs had been discussed over and over again.

"I think of buying a good practice near Southampton, and settling down as a country doctor," he replied. "I have enough property to make me fairly independent, and shall be able to carry on my scientific pursuits without fear of starvation."

"And the next step, I suppose, will be to take a wife?"

"The very next step," replied Everard, looking thoughtfully into the glowing heart of the fire.

Lilian bent her head a little, and caught away a curl at which Mark Antony was snatching. "If no one is going to have any more tea, pussie shall have the rest of the cream," she said.

Cyril, in the mean time, quickly found his way to the well-known room called Lilian's, where Marion was sitting, in the dusk, alone,

but acutely conscious of the light, swift steps
along the corridor which bore her expected
lover to her side. They met in silence, each
young heart being too full for speech; and it
was not until Cyril had released Marion from
his embrace, and placed her in a chair by the
fireside, that he said, kneeling on the rug
near her,

"Am I indeed quite forgiven, Marion?"

"You foolish fellow! How many times
have I written that word?" she replied,
laughing.

"Written, yes; but I want to hear it from
your own lips—I want to be quite sure," he
continued, with unabated earnestness, the
blue fire of his eyes bent upon her soft
brown gaze, while he held both her hands
pressed against his breast.

"Dear Cyril, you make too much of what
is better forgotten," she said. "We quarrelled
long ago and made it up long ago, though
we have not met since."

"Forgotten? Oh, Marion, do you think
I can ever forget? And though you for-

give me, do you think I can ever forgive myself?"

"Certainly. Don't lovers always quarrel; and are they not better friends afterwards? And don't you mean to forgive poor me? I have forgiven us both; though, indeed, those few months were very dreadful."

"Dreadful! They were more than dreadful to me. Oh, Marion, if you knew, if you only dreamed, how unworthy I am, you who are so white, so stainless! You can never guess. Sometimes I wonder that I ever dare hope to call you mine, so black am I in comparison with you."

"Cyril, this is lover's talk—exaggeration. It makes me feel ashamed," she replied, soft blushes stealing over her gentle face in the firelight; "it makes me remember that I am but a weak, foolish girl, and greatly need the guidance of a strong, good man like you."

"Good! God help me!" he exclaimed, turning his face from the modest glance that seemed to scorch his very soul. "Marion,

I am not good; there is no weaker man than I on God's earth, and without you I think I should be utterly lost. Do you know—no, you never can know—what it is to be able to love a good woman; to feel the vileness die out of one at the very thought of her; to be strengthened and purified by the very atmosphere she breathes;—to feel at the thought of losing her—Marion, dear Marion, I think sometimes if you knew the darkness that was upon my soul during those wretched months when we were parted, I fear—oh, I fear that you would cast me off with loathing and scorn——"

Marion smiled a gentle smile, only dimly seeing the passionate agony in Cyril's shadowed face. "I know that I could never scorn *you*," she interrupted, with tender emphasis.

Cyril bent his head over her hands in silence for a few seconds; and then, looking up again, said, in a more collected manner, "Marion, will you take me, worthless as I am, and bear with me and cleave to me through good and evil report, and help me, in spite of the past, to be a better man?"

"Dear," she replied gently, "I have taken you for better and for worse. I don't expect you to be faultless, though I do admire and honour you above all men. I should be sorry if you were faultless, because, you know, I am not faultless myself; I am not like Lilian, even. We shall help each other to be wiser and better, I hope."

Cyril had averted his face from the innocent, loving gaze he could not endure, but he turned once more and looked into Marion's charming face, which was radiant in a sudden burst of firelight, while his own remained in darker shadow than ever. "Promise once more," he said, in low, impassioned tones, "that you will never leave me."

Marion suffered herself to glide into the embrace before her, and repeated the promise, half laughing to herself at the foolish importance assigned to trifles by lovers, and half believing in the intensity of the oft-repeated assurances, and was very happy until a discreet clatter of silver and china was heard outside, followed by a knock at the door, and, after an interval, the entrance of Eliza, who was edified to find Marion at one end of the room, adjusting some china on a bracket, and Cyril at the other, gazing out of the window with great interest at the frosty stars.

When the candles were lighted, the curtains drawn, and the tea poured out, all traces of his passionate agitation had left Cyril's beautiful, severely cut features, and he sat by Marion's side, tea-cup in hand, quiet and content, the very picture of the ideal curate of commonplace just dropped in to tea.

Marion now saw him clearly, and was distressed at his wan and worn appearance, and also at a certain look he never had before the fatal winter she passed in the Mediterranean with her brother. Since then she had met him face to face but once, on the day when he came to ask forgiveness and renew the engagement, and then, naturally, he did not look like his old self. Was it only toil which had robbed Cyril of the bloom

of his youth? she wondered; and she sighed.
" It was time you had a holiday, I think,"
she said softly. " You must not be such an
ascetic any more; you do not belong to a
celibate priesthood, remember."

" This is not exactly the cell of an an-
chorite," replied Cyril, with the smile which
won so many hearts, as he rested his head
comfortably on the back of his low chair,
and gazed upon Marion's slender grace.
" Mayn't I have another lump of sugar,
Marion? Lilian and I have expended much
thought on the decoration of this room."

" And taste," said Marion, looking round
upon the pictures and *bric-à-brac* and various
evidences of cultured taste, though it is not
to be supposed that the two lovers were there
to discuss nothing but the decoration of
Lilian's room.

Cyril had spoken hotly of his dislike to
Marion's Mediterranean tour; and Marion's
pride had been touched till she reminded him
that she was entirely her own mistress, and
might probably continue so to the end of the

chapter. Then ensued a quarrel, only half
serious on either side, a quarrel that a word
or a look would have righted in a moment.
But, unfortunately, Marion had to join her
friends, the Wilmots, sooner than she antici-
pated, and thus hurried off before she could
say good-bye to Cyril and make things
straight with one little smile.

The game of quarrelling, when carried on
between two young, ardent lovers, is a very
pretty diversion, but cannot possibly be
played at a distance, as these two found to
their cost. Deprived of the fairy artillery
of glances, sighs, voices, and gestures, and
confined to the heavy ordnance of letters,
they could not bring things to a happy
conclusion. Letters were first hot, then cold,
then rare, then non-existent, until one day
Cyril wrote, after long silence, to ask Marion
how long she meant to play with his affections. Marion replied that if Cyril considered their engagement as a mere pastime,
the sooner it was broken off the better.
Cyril wrote back to release her from an

engagement which he said he perceived had become distasteful to her.

This was in March.   At Whitsuntide, Everard spent some time at Malbourne, whence Cyril went to Belminster for ordination at Trinity.   He thought Cyril unhappy, and after the ordination he asked him, subsequently to some conversation with Lilian on the subject, if he still cared for Marion, to which Cyril replied in the affirmative.   Then Henry told him that Marion was pining and showing tendencies to consumption.   She was the kind of woman, he said, whose health is perfect in happiness, but who breaks down the moment that elixir of life is denied.   He thought that she loved Cyril still.

Thus emboldened, Cyril owned himself in the wrong, and sued for a return to favour. He could, however, only afford one brief interview with Marion, since he had with some difficulty freed himself from the curacy at Shotover, which had given him a title to deacon's orders, and got himself placed on a

mission staff in the East of London, where
he led a semi-monastic life in a house with
his fellow-curates, and enjoyed to the full the
hard labour for which he had clamoured so
eagerly while at Shotover.

The situation was eminently unfavourable to
courtship, while it seemed to render marriage
absolutely impracticable. Cyril, however,
found a means of reconciling duty with in-
clination, and easily convinced his rector that
his labours would be equally valuable if he
had a home of his own within easy reach of
the scene of his toils, and thus they were to
be married in the spring. The narrow means
which so frequently darken the horizon of
curates' love-dreams had no place in this
romance, since both Cyril and Marion had
wherewithal to keep the wolf from the door.

But they are together at last, and the dark
days which divided them are to be forgotten.

"When I hear the word 'misery,' I think
of last spring," said Marion, laughing.

Cyril's face clouded, and he turned away
and gazed at the fire. "Never think of it!"

he exclaimed, suddenly turning a bright, animated gaze upon Marion. " I shall drive it from your memory, dear, by every act and thought of my life."

Dinner, the hour so fondly welcomed by mortals in general, came all too soon for these ; and, indeed, it was not till the others had taken their places at the table that Marion made her appearance, flushed and charming, and met her brother for the first time since his arrival in the house.

" This is an improvement," he said, holding her at arm's length to look at her, " on the mealy-faced girl I saw three months ago. Pray, miss, where do you get your rouge ? "

" Manufactured on the estate, Henry," replied Mr. Maitland. " Native Malbourne rouge. Let us hope Cyril may acquire some of it."

" It comes off easily," said Everard, gravely, while Cyril became absorbed in Mark Antony, who sat on a stool at Lilian's side at the head of the table, with his chin on a level with the cloth, and who was so enchanted to find himself with a twin on each side of him, that his deep mellifluous purrs threatened to drown the conversation.

"You will be glad to hear that Granfer is still alive and well, and wiser than ever, Henry," said Mrs. Maitland, who was sitting on his right, having, as usual, resigned the head of the table to Lilian.

"I congratulate Malbourne, Mrs. Maitland. It could never go on without Granfer's advice. And the discontented Baines has not yet blown you all up? And friend Wax still wields the ferule in defiance of Lilian?"

"But not in church," said Lilian.

"Because Lilian steals the cane if he brings it," added Marion.

"And is anybody engaged, or born, or dead?" continued Everard, gaily. "By the way, what has happened to Ben Lee? It struck me that he had been drinking this afternoon. And our friend Alma, how is she?"

There was a dead silence for a second or

two, and Everard's eager gaze of inquiry met no response from the eyes bent resolutely on the plates.

"Let me send you some more beef, Henry," said Mr. Maitland, looking up from his joint with sudden briskness. "Come, where is your boasted appetite? Yes, bring Dr. Everard's plate, Eliza."

"But Alma? Oh, I hope there is nothing wrong with her?" continued Everard, looking round with a dismayed gaze, while Mrs. Maitland laid her hand warningly on his sleeve. "Oh, Lilian, Alma is not dead?"

"Worse," replied Lilian, in a low voice— "far worse."

There were tears, he saw, trembling upon her eyelashes; and if ever tears resembled pearls, then, he thought, did those precious drops, and if ever mortal woman was dear, then was Lilian. He saw it all now on the instant, and he remembered how much Lilian had done for Alma, and how at Whitsuntide she had spoken of her and cared about her absence from the Sacrament, and so dismayed was he by this catastrophe that, having none of the ready resources and fine tact which ensure social success, he simply, like the honest, clumsy fellow he was, dropped his knife and fork, and gazed horror-struck before him. Fortunately, at that moment Lennie, who was stretched on the hearthrug, intent upon "Ivanhoe," bethought himself of an important event, and took advantage of the silence to proclaim it.

"I say, Henry," he exclaimed, "what do you think? I'm going into trousers to-morrow."

"Why, it was all over Oldport," said Cyril. "Bills in every window. 'Oh yes! oh yes! oh yes! Know all by these presents that Lennie Maitland goes into trousers to-morrow.'"

"Oh, won't I smack you by-and-by!" observed Lennie, tranquilly returning to the gests of Brian de Bois-Guilbert.

"I think, Cyril, you scarcely appreciate the honour your brother intends you," said Mr. Maitland. "He dons these virile garments for the purpose of hearing your sermon. He evidently holds trousers to be conducive to a pious frame of mind, or at least to a certain mental receptivity ; eh, Lennie, lad ? "

" The unfortunate tailor's life has been a burden to him in the fear that the suit would not be ready in time," said Mrs. Maitland.

" In time to hear Cywil pweach," added Marion, laughing.

" How many times have they been tried on, Lennie ? " asked Lilian.

" Never you mind their rubbish," said Everard ; " ask Miss Mawion how often she calls me Henwy ? "

" And Cywil will line the pockets with silver for you," added Cyril, who was looking very happy, having, as Eliza observed with satisfaction, his hand locked in Marion's under the tablecloth.

No sooner had the ladies withdrawn, than Everard burst out, " And who is the scoundrel ? "

" Softly, softly, Henry ! beware of rash judgments," returned Mr. Maitland, whose face took a grieved look. " Nothing is known, which is hateful to me because of the great wave of scandal and the dreadful scorching of tongues which arises about the matter. Lee, I know not why, assumes that it is a gentleman; and public opinion, and, I fear I must add, his reputation, point to Ingram Swaynestone. Sir Lionel has spoken to him, but he absolutely denies it ; and, indeed—— "

"In short," broke in Cyril, who was extremely busy with some walnuts on his plate, " the less said about these miserable scandals the better."

" True, quite true," said his father, with a heavy sigh.

" But Alma! the little girl we used to play with at the Temple, with Lilian, and often Ingram, and the girl Swaynestones ! " cried Henry. "I cannot believe any wrong of her. She has been wronged—of that I am sure."

" Truly, I had never dreamed of such trouble for Alma, poor child! " said Mr. Maitland. " Elsewhere in the parish, of course,

one dreads such things, knowing their temptations.   It is a heavy grief for me, Henry,
as you may imagine."

"And for Lilian," added Everard.   "Yes,
I know how you love your spiritual children,
sir, and can imagine your distress.   And poor
Lee, he was so proud of her.   He is sullen, I
see; a sure sign of grief.   Oh, I hope he is
not unkind to her!"

"The stepmother is hard, and has a sharp
tongue!   She forgets what poor Alma did
for her child.   Altogether, it is a sad, sad
history.   The Temple, I suppose, holds more
unhappiness than any house in the county."

"Oh, really, my dear father," exclaimed
Cyril, who seemed pained beyond endurance,
"you must not take it so to heart!   She is
not the first——"

"By Jove, Maitland!" interrupted Everard,
"you are the last man from whom I should
expect an echo of Mephistopheles.   He never
said anything more diabolical than that—' Sie
ist die Erste nicht.'"

Cyril coloured so hotly that he exhibited

the phenomenon of a black blush, while Mr. Maitland hastened to say that Cyril was in a different position from Faust, who had wrought the wrong. " And then," he added, " Cyril is doubtless weary of sin and sorrow, of which, in his parish, he must have far more than we in our simple rustic home have any idea of, busy as Satan undoubtedly is every-where."

" Quite so," returned Cyril, wearily. " My words sounded unfortunately, Everard ; but, as my father suggests, when one has break-fasted and lunched for weeks upon peccant parishioner, one does not enjoy the same dish at dinner."

Everard's rejoinder was prevented by the intrusion of a sunny head at the door, and the clear voice of Winnie was heard crying, ' Do make haste ! Me and Lennie want to know what is in that basket, and Lilian won't let us." Whereupon Cyril sprang up and chased the delighted child through the hall and into the drawing-room, where she took refuge, screaming, in Lilian's dress.

The basket which so stimulated the children's curiosity was well known to contain the young men's Christmas gifts to the family, and was forthwith uncovered amid a scene of joyous turbulence, and had its contents distributed.

The task of collecting the parcels in the basket and conveying them to the drawing-room had been performed by Eliza with thrills of delicious agony, for it was almost beyond human nature not to take at least one peep at a packet containing the very ribbon she longed for, and at another revealing glimpses of a perfect love of a shawl, which proved to be destined for cook. However, she appeared with a perfectly demure countenance when fetched by Lennie, with the other maids, to receive her presents. By that time Mr. Maitland had become lost to all earthly cares, in an arm-chair, with an old battered volume Everard had picked up at a book-stall in Paris for him ; Winnie was wondering if some fairy had informed Henry that a fishing-rod of her very own had been her soul's unattainable star for months; and Lennie was dancing round the room with an illustrated "Don Quixote" clasped in his arms.

It was pleasant to see Cyril making his gifts. Each was offered with a suitable word, tender or droll, according to the recipient, and with a grace that an emperor might have envied, though a carping observer would have detected that the gifts themselves had been purchased as nearly as possible at the same shop. As for Everard, he made his offerings with a sneaking air, and seemed glad to get them off his hands. He threw the "Don Quixote" at Lennie, with "Here, you scamp!" and placed the invalid reading-stand by Mrs. Maitland, with an awkward, "I don't know if this thing will be any good to you."

"Why, Henry, who told you that father's life has been a burden to him for months for want of that old edition?" asked Lilian.

"He is a wizard; he should be burnt," laughed Cyril, reflecting inwardly that while his gifts cost money, Everard's cost time and thought and infinite trouble in hunting out.

"But ain't Lilian to have anything?" inquired the ingenuous Lennie; for Lilian and Cyril never gave each other presents—they had things so much in common, and Everard appeared to have forgotten her.

Lilian appealed, as usual, to Mark Antony for sympathy, and Everard grew very hot, while Cyril absorbed himself in fitting the bracelet he had given to Marion upon her slender arm. Then Lilian looked up.

"It was horrid of you to forget me, Henry," she said.

"I didn't forget you," stammered Everard; "but the thing was so trifling I hadn't the courage—— It's only a photograph of the picture which inspired Browning's 'Guardian Angel.' Here it is, if you think it worth having. You said you would give anything to see Guercino's picture at Fano."

"Oh, Henry, how very kind and thoughtful of you!" exclaimed Lilian, her face transfigured with pleasure. "But I thought there was no photograph?"

"Well, no; but young Stobart was doing Italy in the autumn, and I got him to go to Fano with his camera. It wasn't far out of his way," he replied, in a tone of apology.

Lennie's solicitude being relieved, he and the others were absorbed each after his own fashion; no one observed these two. Lilian looked up at Henry, who had thrown himself into a low chair by her side, so that their faces were on a level. Her eyes were dewy and bright; they gazed straight into his for a minute, and then fell. "You had it done for me," she murmured.

It was the crowning moment of Everard's happy night. He bent over the spirit-like hand resting on the cat; and unseen pressed his lips to it. He knew that Lilian loved him, and knew that he loved her. He said nothing more; it was enough bliss for one day.

CHAPTER VII.

BEFORE going to rest that night, Mr. Maitland led Everard to his study, and there subjected him to a searching cross-examination on the subject of Cyril's care-worn and unhealthy appearance, which Everard referred to his overzeal in his labours, and the excessive austerities which he practised.

"It would be all very well for him to mortify his flesh if he had too much of it to balance his spirit," Everard observed; "but, as a matter of fact, he has too little."

"Cyril is sensitive," his father replied; "his nerves are too tensely strung, like those of all extremely refined and poetic natures. We thought, Lilian and I, that it was the estrangement from Marion which was preying . on him. It was that which caused him to leave Shotover, and plunge into this terrific London work—that and, of course, higher motives."

"Cyril, though healthy, is delicate," replied Everard. "He ought never to fast; he cannot bear it, especially when working. His brain will give way under such discipline. Observe him to-morrow when he preaches. There is too much nervous excitement."

The next morning Cyril did not appear till the end of breakfast, and then took nothing but a cup of coffee.

"Really, Cyril, I did think Sunday at least was a feast-day!" cried Everard, pausing in his own manful assault on a well-piled plate of beef.

"But Cyril is to celebrate to-day; he must fast," Lilian explained; and then Everard observed that Mr. Maitland's breakfast consisted of nothing, and groaned within himself, and asked his friends if they considered it decorous for clergymen to faint in the midst of public worship.

"When a man has to work, he should feed

himself into proper condition," he said to unheeding ears.

After breakfast, the Maitland family re-
paired in a body to the Sunday school, and
Everard went out to smoke a pipe alone, and,
the frost being keen, he wore an overcoat,
finding one of his own in the hall. He had
some difficulty in putting it on, and could not
by any means induce it to meet across the
chest. This gave him great satisfaction.
" It cannot be that my Sunday-go-to-meeting
clothes take up so much room," he mused.
" No; I am increasing in girth round the
chest. Who could imagine that one night's
happiness and country air would produce such
an effect ? A new scientific fact."

It was pleasant on the lawn in the frosty
Sunday stillness. The sunbeams danced on
the evergreens and smiled on the Shotover
parklands ; a robin sang its cheerfully
pathetic song ; and a flock of rooks uttered
their breezy caws in the pale blue above his
head. Everard smoked with profound enjoyment ; he thought of last night's enchant-

ment, and the promise he had just extracted from Lilian to sit with him in the Rectory pew instead of with the school-children. His hands were thrust for warmth into his coat-pockets, and in one of them he felt the square outline of a letter, which he drew out, wondering—since his habits were neat and methodical, as became a student of natural science—how he came to leave a letter there. The letter, however, had no envelope and no address. He opened it, and found, in the half-formed, clear writing of an unlearned person, probably some patient in humble life, the following :—

"No, I will never, never marry you. What good could that do me, now you do not love me no more—me that loved you better than Heaven and her own poor soul? Would I like to see you miserable, and spoil your prospex? To marry the likes of me would ruin you, and how could that make me happy? Marry *her*; it is better for you. I have done wrong for love of you, and God

will punish me.   But you are sorry, and will
be forgiven.   Farewell for ever.

" Your broken-hearted

" A."

The gracious light of the wintry morning
seemed to fade out of the pale pure sky;
there was no more delight in the robin's
song; the bright crystals of the hoar-frost
sparkled in vain for Everard.   "Why, why
are there such things?" he murmured.
" Why was Cyril's echo of Mephistopheles
so much more poignant in its cynicism
because of its truth ?"

The weak suffering, the strong going scot-
free; Alcestis plunging, love-radiant, into the
darkness of Hades, while Admetus rejoices in
the light of heaven; women trusting, and
men deceiving—what a world!   All the confused misery of the painful insoluble riddle of
earth seemed to awake and trouble the clear
happiness of Everard's soul at the story told
in the poor little scrap of paper, the more
pathetic for its bad spelling and artless

grammar. And how came such an epistle in his pocket? Doubtless some friend had borrowed his coat; some heedless rackety medical student, perchance, and flavoured it with tobacco and correspondence. " Sie ist die Erste nicht," the rooks seemed to say in their pleasant, fresh morning caws.

But now the bells came chiming slowly on the clear air, those dear, drowsy three strokes which awoke in his heart so many echoes of home and boyhood and sweet innocent life beneath the beloved roof where Lilian dwelt; bells calling people to come and pray, to think of God and heaven, and forsake all the sin and sorrow of the troubled earth—calling people to hear how even such black things as the letter told of might be made white again like snow; to hear the kind fatherly counsels of such as Mr. Maitland or Cyril. And his heart swelled when he thought that Cyril had devoted his stainless youth, his bright promise, and his splendid gifts to a calling which, however vainly, tried to stem the tide of all this mad, sad evil, and lift men out of the mire of earth's misery. How beautiful to have Cyril's faith, and the power of thus consecrating himself! How poor in comparison his own career, devoted merely to the healing of men's bodies, to the satisfaction of noble desire for knowledge, and the widening the horizon of men's thoughts!

Like all thinkers, and especially those whose thoughts dwell much on the study of natural facts, Everard had many doubts, and often feared that the Christianity so dear to him through instinct, training, and association, might be, after all, but a fairy dream. But the atmosphere of Malbourne, and more especially the influence of Mr. Maitland's genuine and practical piety, together with Cyril's bright enthusiasm, quenched these doubts as nothing else could; and now the village bells fell like balm on his troubled soul, and he responded with cheery good temper to Lennie, who came bounding over the lawn in the proud consciousness of trousers, crying, "Come along, Henry, and look at Lilian's donkey."

He thrust the paper in his pocket, and, taking the little fellow's hand, trotted off with him towards Winnie, who was approaching them at headlong pace, with curls streaming in the wind, and soon seized his other hand, and led him to the meadow, where he beheld one of the sorriest beasts he had ever set eyes on, cropping the frosty grass, and winking lazily in the sun.

"What can Lilian do with such a creature?" he asked.

"Oh, she makes it happy, like all her things," replied Lennie. "Won't you stare when you see her three-legged cat, and the fox with the broken leg she has in the stable!"

"She likes hurt things," commented Winnie, while Lennie related how Lilian met this donkey one day in the road leading over the downs. It was harnessed to a cart laden with vegetables, and had fallen between the shafts, where its owner, a brutal, bad fellow, well known in Malbourne, was furiously belabouring it.

"Didn't he stare when Lilian caught him

by the collar and pulled him off the donkey!"
said Lennie. "Then he fell all of a tremble,
and Lilian told him he would be sent to
prison or fined. And he said he was too
poor to buy another donkey, and couldn't
help this one growing old and weak. So
Lilian gave him ten shillings for it."

"Dear Lilian!" Everard said to himself, as
he looked at the wretched beast, with its stiff
limbs and body scarred by old sores and
stripes. "Which do you love best, Winnie,
Lilian or Cyril?"

"Cyril," replied both children, unhesi-
tatingly, but could give no reason for their
preference, until Lennie, after long cogitation,
said, "He does make a fellow laugh so."

Everard smiled, and thought of Words-
worth's boy with his weathercock. The day
was warmer now, and bidding Lennie run
indoors with his great coat, he set off to
church with the children.

It was a matter of time for a person of
any consideration to get through Malbourne
Churchyard, for there, grouped upon either

side the porch, lounged a little crowd of Malbourne worthies, solemnly passing the churchgoers in review, and headed, of course, by Granfer in a clean white smock-frock, and with his hale old many-coloured visage and veined hands looking purplish in the frosty air. Tom Hale was there, making a bright centre to the cool-toned picture in his red tunic and spotless, well-brushed clothes; while Jim, with open breast and sailor garb, lent a bit of picturesque that not even the Sunday coats of Baines's manufacture could quite subdue.

Lennie held up his head, and felt that his trousers were making a deep impression; while Everard stopped and wished a good morning to them all, smock-frocks, Sunday coats, and uniforms, and received a little dignified patronage from Granfer, who had always regarded him with some disparagement, as being neither a Swaynestone nor a Maitland, but a mere appendage to the latter family, a circumstance which helped to render Granfer the delight of Everard's life.

The present moment did not find Granfer conversational, his mental powers being concentrated on observing the animated scene before him. There was Farmer Long, with his wife and daughters in their warm scarlets and purples, to scrutinize as they strolled along the road and over the church-yard path; then the more distant farmers, who drove up to the lych-gate in old-fashioned gigs, and, having dropped their families, hastened to the Sun to put up the strong, coarse-limbed horses; then came the Garretts from Northover, new people, whom Mal-bourne regarded, with a mixture of scorn and envy, as mere mushroom pretenders. They came on foot, their own gates being but a stone's-throw from the church, a hand-some family of sons and daughters, coeval with the Maitlands. To them Granfer's salutation was almost infinitesimal in its elaborate graduation. Then, blending with the drowsy chime of the three bells, arose the clatter of hoofs and the roll of wheels, and the Swaynestone laudau, with its splendid

high-stepping horses, swept easily up to the
gate, the silver-mounted harness, the silken
coats of the steeds, the panels, and the re-
volving wheel-spokes flashing in the sun.
Granfer did not know it, but perhaps he
dimly felt that the splendour of this apparition somehow enlarged and beautified the
dim, narrow horizon of his life.

Ben Lee's very livery, not to speak of his
skilful and effective driving, contributed
vaguely to Granfer's importance; as also did
the courteous elegance and finely built form
of Sir Lionel, and the manner in which, the
footman having retired at a look, he handed
out Lady Swaynestone and his daughter
Ethel, in their velvets and furs. But Granfer
was distressed to see that Ben Lee no longer
drove up with his former dash, and turned
his shining steeds in the direction of the Sun
with no more consequence than if he had
been driving a mere brewer's dray. " Ah,
Ben ain't the man he was ! " he muttered,
after having helped Sir Lionel and his
family with the sunshine of his approbation
into church.

Then came the tripping, whispering procession of school-children, led by the rector, followed by Wax, who was involved in the double misery of new Sunday broadcloth and the absence of his cane, without which emblem of authority he was ever a lost man; and last of all came Cyril, who found time for a word and a smile for each of the group, and left them all exhilarated by his passing presence as if by a draught of wine. Then the bells ceased, the loungers entered the church, and Granfer himself, the sunshine warming his wintry white hair, walked slowly with the aid of his stout oak staff up the centre aisle to his allotted place.

He was already seated, and Cyril's musical voice had given a deeper pathos to the sentence, " Hide thy face from my sins," when Ingram Swaynestone and his sister Maude entered, rosy and fresh from their long brisk walk in the frosty morning. Ingram Swaynestone was tall and fair and strongly built, the typical young Englishman, who belongs to no class and only one country, physically perfect, good-tempered, and well-spoken, with a perfect digestion and a nervous system undistraught by intellectual burdens and riddles of the painful earth. His appearance with his pretty, fair-haired sister caused a tiny stir, almost imperceptible, like a summer breath through ripe corn, amongst the fairer portion of the congregation, with whom he was extremely popular, not only on account of his good looks and known appreciation of feminine charms, but also because of a faint delicious aroma of wickedness that hung about his name.

The devotions of several undoubtedly pious young maidens were more than once interrupted for the purpose of looking to see if he was looking, which he certainly was at every one of them in turn, when opportunity permitted; while Cyril's beautiful voice rang through the church, and Everard and Lilian, who had always loved and admired the simple majesty of the Liturgy, felt that they had never before known its real beauty.

When he read of the Massacre of the

Innocents, one or two women cried. The tone in which he read that Rachel was weeping for her children and would not be comforted, poignantly reminded them that they could never be comforted for their lost little ones buried outside in the sunny churchyard. Henry, and Lilian, and Marion, and the children all gazed up with admiring affection at the beautiful young priest standing white-robed outside the chancel at the eagle lectern, Henry thinking that the music of Cyril's voice alone surpassed any chanted cathedral service.

Often in after-years did Henry and Lilian think of that sweet Sunday morning with refreshment: the solemn beauty of the old church, with its heavy Norman arches; the sunshine stealing in, mellow and soft, through the south windows and tingeing the snowy frock of Granfer, who sat just below the chancel, and leant forward on his staff in an attitude of rapt attention; the innocent looks of the choir-boys, amongst whom was Dicky Stevens, fourth in descent from Granfer, and whom Lilian had delivered from the tyranny of the rod; and Mr. Maitland's reverend aspect, as he bent his silvered head and listened to Cyril's pure voice.

But the moment which lingered in his heart's memory till his dying day was that in which he knelt with Marion and Lilian and the villagers at the altar, and received the holy symbols from Cyril's own consecrated hands. He never forgot Cyril's pale, saint-like features and white-stoled form, the crimson from a martyr's robe in the south chancel window staining in a long bar the priest's breast and hands and the very chalice he held.

"I was so glad," Lilian said, when they were walking home together, Marion having stopped to speak to some one, "to see you there, Henry, because Cyril is often troubled about your daring speculations."

"Your father never fails to still my doubts, Lilian," he replied. "There is that in his plain, unpretending sermons, which carries conviction straight into one's heart. Sermons, as a rule, simply bore me; but Mr. Maitland's—— Well, you know, he always was my *beau idéal* of a parish priest."

Lilian's face kindled. " You are the only person who really appreciates my father," she replied. " Even Cyril does not quite know what gifts he has buried in this tiny rustic place, and willingly and consciously buried."

" I honour his intellect, but still more his heart, which speaks not only in his studiously plain sermons, but even more in his life. Cyril could take no better model."

" True; yet we all think Cyril destined to something higher," replied Lilian.

" By the way, Henry," said Cyril at luncheon, " I took your overcoat by mistake this morning. I hope it didn't put you out much; my things are all too small for you."

" That fellow is always appropriating my property, and I am too big to retaliate," growled Everard, who had forgotten all about the tight overcoat of the morning.

" Oh, I say, Cywil," broke in Lennie,

" wasn't Ingwam Swaynestone in a wage with you for not pweaching this morning ! He came to church on purpose, and he does hate going to church in the winter, he says, because the cold nips the girls' noses and makes them look so ugly."

" He doesn't mean that nonsense, Lennie," said Mr. Maitland, laughing gently. " He pays his rector a fine compliment, to say the least of it," he added.

Cyril, who was by no means making up for his morning fast, looked as if he thought Ingram was more likely to be interested in the colour of girls' noses than the quality of any sermons. Then he learnt how Ingram had called with offers of guns and horses to Everard and himself, and had been at play with Winnie, who was now in dire disgrace and condemned to go without pudding, in consequence of having made Ingram's nose bleed.

" Oh, really, mother ! " he exclaimed, stroking the bright curls brushing his arms, " isn't that rather hard ? Winnie did not mean it; it might have been her nose. Do you think Ingram will go without pudding, Win? Let her off, mother. I never saw a little girl behave better in church."

Whereupon Winnie was respited, after many comments from her elders on her rough ways and romping habits and constant breakages, which, it appeared, were a source of perennial disgrace to the little girl.

Cyril had very tender ways with children, and was almost as sorry for hurt things as Lilian. That very afternoon a child stumbled and fell on the way to church, and Everard saw him slip aside in his long cassock, and pick up the howling, dust-covered urchin with some merry, tender observation, wipe away the tears and blood with his own spotless handkerchief before Wax had time to bring out a denunciation on the brat's heedlessness, and comfort him finally with pence, though the parson's bell had rung, and Mrs. Wax had come to the end of her voluntary on the harmonium, and begun over again in despair.

The morning congregation had received some additions, to wit, those lazy sabbatarians who kept their day of rest so literally as to get up too late to go to church in the morning, those mothers too fatigued by performing the family toilettes to perform their own, and those who cooked the Sunday dinners and minded the babies, the majority of which latter accompanied their parents to afternoon service. It was pleasant, too, to observe that Ingram Swaynestone's piety had conquered his pain at the eclipse of feminine beauty, and that he helped to swell the little crowd.

When Cyril ascended the pulpit, he looked round the dim church with an anxious, searching gaze, and Lilian observed that his eye rested with apprehension on the Lees' pew, and he appeared relieved when he saw Mrs. Lee standing there alone. Then he glanced in the direction of the Swaynestone servants' pew, where Ben Lee sat, glum and downcast, and Judkins, with a haggard look, held his hymn-book before his face. They

were singing " Hark, the herald angels,"
Job Stubbs and Dickie Stevens bringing out
the treble with a will, and the basses bearing
their parts manfully.

Cyril distinguished all the voices—those of
Lilian and Everard, Marion and the children,
Sir Lionel and his daughters, the Rectory
maids, the smock-frocks, Tom and Jim Hale,
Baines, the tailor, who was only an occasional
church-goer, and loved to air his bass occasionally in orthodox ears—he heard even
Granfer's own tremulous quaver, which had
been a tenor of local celebrity, and a crowd
of young memories rushed over him. He
clutched the edge of the pulpit, regardless of
the holly-wreath which encircled it, and
pricked his fingers, and, when the last notes
of " Herald angels " died away in the final
quaver of an old woman half a bar behind,
was silent for a few moments.

At last he recovered himself, and gave out
his text—" Keep innocency, and take heed to
the thing that is right, for that shall bring a
man peace at the last."

He felt them all gazing up at him—Lennie
and Winnie, with their innocent eyes and
mouths wide open to hear " Cywil pweach ; "
his mother, who seldom ventured to church ;
Farmer Long and his family ; the well-known
villagers ; Granfer, with his head on one
side, like an old bird, the better to hear him ;
Ben Lee—yes, Ben Lee was looking ; his
father in the chancel was looking also.

Cyril turned pale ; Marion caught her
breath, but was soon quieted by the clear,
pure notes of the young preacher's voice.
He could not but pause, he said, before that
congregation, and question himself deeply
and sternly before he presumed to address
them. They had seen him grow up among
them. Many were his elders, had held him
in their arms, chidden the faults of his boyhood, taught him, cared for him ; many had
been his playmates and companions, known
his weaknesses, shared, perchance, in his
escapades. How should he speak to them ?

Everard disapproved of these personal remarks ; and yet, when he heard the silver

tones of Cyril's voice, his easy flowing
sentences, and the delicacy of his allusions,
he could not but be charmed. The fact was,
as he reflected, that Cyril could do what no
other man might, and still charm. His very
faults and weaknesses were, in a manner,
endearing.

He felt it, nevertheless, a great privilege,
he continued, to be placed there, and he
asked of their patience to hear him, for the
sake of his office. Then, referring to his
manuscript, he briefly touched upon the story
of the martyred innocents and its lessons;
and not till then did the profound snore
of William Grove and other accustomed
sleepers arise. Every creature had kept
awake during the unaccustomed prologue,
and, indeed, many of the habitual sleepers
were still awake, considering it only fair to
Mr. Cyril. Then the preacher spoke of the
beauty of innocence, and his manner, hitherto
so quiet, changed, and became more and more
impassioned, till some of the sleepers woke
and gazed about them with dazed wonder,

as the tones of that clarion voice besought
them all to keep innocency, that pearl beyond
all price, that one costly treasure without
which there was no light in the summer
sun, nor any joy in youth and spring-time.
Then he painted the tortures of a guilty
conscience, the agony beyond all agonies,
with such power and passion, and such a
richness of poetic diction and picturesque
imagery, that many a man trembled, some
women sobbed, and poor Ben Lee uttered a
stifled groan.

Everard grew uncomfortable. He began
to fear some unseemly hysteric excitement
in the little congregation, and was distressed
to find Marion and Mrs. Maitland crying
without reserve. Lilian's eyes were moist,
but she did not cry; she was pale with a
reflection of Cyril's white passion. Mr.
Maitland covered his face with his surplice.
He too was uneasy, and more affected than
he liked to acknowledge to himself; yet he
hoped that Alma's betrayer might be present
and have his heart touched. The dusk was

falling fast in the dim, deep-shadowed building; two or three sparks of light glowed among the white robes of the choir, and up among the dark arches Cyril's face showed haggard and agonized in the little isle of light made by the two pale tapers on each side of him in the darkness.

Long did the little congregation remember that scene: the hush of attention, broken only by an occasional sob from some woman— for most of the sleepers were awake now, and dimly conscious of the unaccustomed passion breaking the drowsy air around them—the great growing shadows in the fast-darkening church; the mass of awe-struck faces pale in the grey gloom; the rosy gleams of the scattered tapers on the choristers' surplices; and up above them, from the heart of the mysterious darkness, the one beautiful, impassioned face in the lonely radiance, and the mighty musical voice pealing forth the unutterable anguish of sin; and the light which subsequent events threw upon it only rendered it the more impressive.

"It is true, indeed," said the preacher, suddenly easing the intolerable tension of his passion, and speaking in calmer tones, "that what a holy writer has called 'the princely heart of innocence,' may be regained after long anguish of penitence and prayer, but the consequences of sin roll on in ever-growing echoes, terrible with the thunder of everlasting doom; the contrite heart is utterly broken, and the life for ever saddened and marred. Innocence once lost, my brethren, the old careless joy of youth never returns. O thou, whosoever thou be, man, woman, or even child; thou who hast once stained thy soul with deadly sin, 'not poppy, nor mandragora, nor all the drowsy syrups of the world, shall ever medicine thee to that sweet sleep which thou ow'dst yesterday.'

"Yet despair not, beloved brethren," he added, with flute-like softness, for his voice had again risen in agonized intensity; "there is forgiveness and healing for all. But oh! keep innocency, keep innocency; guard and treasure that inestimable, irrecoverable pos-

session, that pure perennial source of joyous
days and peaceful nights, and take heed, take
watchful heed, of the thing that is right. Keep
innocency, O little children, sitting here in the
holy church this evening, beneath the eyes
of those who love and guard you—you whose
souls are yet fresh with the dew of baptism,
keep, oh, keep your innocency! Keep it,
youths and children, who wear the chorister's
white robe! Keep innocency, young men
and maidens, full of heart and hope; keep
this one pearl, I pray you, for there is no
joy without it! And you, men and women
of mature years, strong to labour and bowed
with cares and toils innumerable—you who,
in the hurry of life's hot noon, have scarce
time to think of heaven, with its white robes
and peace, yet see that you keep innocency
through all! And you, standing amid the
long golden lights of life's evening, aged
men and women who wear the honoured
crown of white hairs, watch still, and see that
you guard your priceless treasure even to
the last. Keep innocency, I conjure you,

for that shall bring a man peace at the last! Peace, peace," he repeated, with a yearning intensity that culminated in a deep, hard sob, " peace!"

He paused, and there was dense silence for some seconds, and Everard saw that the blue brilliance of his eyes was blurred with tears; while Sir Lionel and Ingram experienced a sense of profound relief in the hope that the too-exciting sermon was at an end. The congregation rose joyously to their feet, eased of a strain that was becoming intolerable.

When Cyril had left the pulpit, his father pronounced the benediction on the kneeling crowd in his calm, sweet tones, so restful after the storm and passion of the young preacher's richly compassed voice. But the blessing did not reach Cyril's distracted soul. Taking advantage of the shadows when he reached his place in the chancel, he glided swiftly behind the pillars, like some hurt spirit fleeing from the benison that would heal it, till he reached the vestry, where he threw himself in a chair behind a screen, and covered his face. When Mr. Maitland in due time followed the choir thither, he did not at first observe the silent, ghostly figure in the shadow; and then becoming aware of him, he left him to himself till the choristers were gone, thinking that he was praying. But on approaching nearer, he was startled to hear strong sobs issue from the veiled figure.

"My dear boy," he remonstrated, "this will never do. Too much excitement is unwholesome both for priest and people. Come, master yourself, dear lad. You are unwell; this fasting is not wise. Henry was right."

"Oh, father," sobbed Cyril, "it is not the fasting! Oh, shut the door, and let us be alone, and let me tell you all—all!"

"Come, come," said the gentle old man; "calm yourself, and tell me whatever you like later. At present we are both worn out, and need change of thought. You have a great gift, dear fellow, and I trust your words have struck home to at least one conscience——"

"They have—oh, they have, indeed!" repeated Cyril, with increasing agitation; "and that miserable conscience—— Oh, father, father! how can I tell you——?"

"Hush! hush! This is hysteria, as Everard predicted. Say no more; I insist upon your silence. Remember where we are! Drink this water. Stay! I will call Henry;" and Mr. Maitland went quickly into the church, where Everard was yet lingering with Lilian, who always had various errands connected with the parish to transact in the porch, and beckoned him to the vestry.

Cyril did not resist his father's will any more, but sank back with a moan, half of anguish, half of relief, and listened meekly to the rough kindliness of Everard and the gentle remonstrances of his father.

"This is a pretty scene, Mr. Maitland," observed Everard, on entering the vestry. "Ill? Of course he is ill, after exciting himself on an empty stomach! The end of such goings-on as these, my friend, is Bedlam. Take this brandy, and then go quietly home and get a good sleep, and let us have no more of this nonsense, for goodness sake."

So Cyril did as they bid him, and held his peace. Had he but acted on his heart's impulse, and spoken out then as he wished, he would have produced sorrow and dismay indeed, but the long, lingering tragedy which was to involve so many lives would have been for ever averted.

Once, perhaps, in each crisis of our lives, our guardian angel stands before us with his hands full of golden opportunity, which, if we grasp, it is well with us; but woe to us if we turn our backs sullenly on our gentle visitor, and scorn his celestial gift! Never again is the gracious treasure offered, and the favourable moment returns no more.

CHAPTER VIII.

"Ay, you med all mark my words!" said
Granfer, looking solemnly round from under
the shadow of his bushy grey eyebrows.
"I've a zaid it, and I'll zay it agen—ay, that
I 'ool, let they go agen it as may! You med
all mark my words, I zay. Queen Victòree'll
make he a bishop avore she's done wi' 'un."

"Ay," chorused the listening group, who
were standing around the village oracle in
the churchyard, looking phantom-like in the
pale blending of sunset and moonrise; and
then there was a thoughtful pause, during
which Granfer's shrewd grey eyes scrutinized
each face with an air of challenge.

"Ter'ble vine praiching zure-ly," observed
Hale, the wheelwright.

"Vine! you med well zay that," rejoined

Granfer, sternly. " I tell 'ee all, there never was praiching that vine in all Malbourne lands avore! Ay, I've a zaid it, and I'll zay it agen ! "

" Made me sweat, 'ee did," observed Straun, the blacksmith, whose Sunday appearance was a caricature on his burly working-day presentment; for broadcloth of Baines's rough fashioning now hid the magnificent muscular arms and bare neck; a tall hat, too small in the head, replaced the careless, smoke-browned cap of every day; and the washing and shaving to which his face had been subjected gave it an almost unnatural pallor.

" Ye med well sweat, Jarge Straun, when you thinks on yer zins," reflected Granfer, piously.

" 'Twas ter'ble vine; but darned if I knows what 'twas all about ! " said William Grove, scratching his curly head with some perplexity.

" Ah ! Mr. Cyril, he have a dale too much larning for the likes o' you, Willum," returned Granfer, graciously condescending to

William's weaker intellect; "let he alone
for that. Why, Lard love 'ee, Willum, *I*
couldn't make out more'n a quarter on't
mezelf; that I couldn't, I tell 'ee! A vast
o' larning in that lad's head."

" Ay, and some on it was poetry; I yerd
the jingle of it," said sailor Jim.

" Master, now," continued Granfer, settling
himself more comfortably against a tombstone,
and leaning forward on his stick—" Lard 'a
massey, any vool med unnerstand he! He
spakes in his discoorses jest as though he
was a zitting in front of vire atop of a
cricket, and a zaying, ' Well, Granfer, and
how be the taäties a-coming up?' or, ' Granfer,
think o' yer zins avore you blames other
volk.' Ay, that's how he spakes, bless 'un!
He don't know no better, he don't. Can't
spake no grander than the Lard have give
'un grace to."

" Master's a good man," said Straun,
defiantly. " He've a done his duty by we
this thirty year."

" Ay, he's well enough, master is," continued Granfer, in a tolerant manner; "I never had no vault to vind wi' he, bless 'un! A vine vamily he've had, too! He've a done so well as he could; but a never was no praicher to spake on, I tell 'ee."

"Ter'ble pretty what Mr. Cyril said about preaching to them as knowed him a boy," said Tom Hale. "Them esskypades, now," he added fondly, as he caressed his moustache and struck one of his martial attitudes.

"What's a esskypade, Granfer?" inquired a smock-frock.

"A esskypade," returned Granfer, slowly and thoughtfully—"a esskypade, zo to zay, is, in a way o' spaking, what you med call a zet-to—a zart of a scrimmage like;" and he fixed his glittering eye fiercely, yet half doubtfully, on Tom Hale's face, as much as to challenge him to deny it.

"Just so," responded Tom. "I said to meself, I said, 'Mr. Cyril is thinking of the set-to we had together in father's yard that Saturday afternoon; that's what he means by his esskypades.'"

"Ay, and you licked him well," added Jim, eagerly; "that was summat like a fight, Tom."

"Master Cyril had to be carried home, and kep' his bed for a week; and Tom, he couldn't see out of his eyes next day," commented the elder Hale, with pride in his brother's prowess.

"Ay, you dreshed 'un, zure enough, Tom," commented Granfer, graciously.

"He took a deal of licking, and hit out like a man," said the modest warrior, who loved Cyril with the profound affection inspired only by a vanquished foe.

Tom had fought sterner battles since. He had been through the Indian Mutiny campaign, and known the grim realities of Lucknow; but his heart still glowed, as he saw before him, in his mind's eye, the prostrate form of Cyril on the grass among the timber of the wheelwright's yard—poor, vanquished Cyril, slighter, though older, than himself, with his little shirt torn and blood-stained—and heard the applause of his comrades gathered to watch the fray.

" Well, I minds 'n, a little lad, chivying
Granfer's wuld sow round meadow," struck
in Stevens, who had now completed all his
duties in the church and locked the door,
the great key of which he carried in his
hand.

" A vine, peart buoy as ever I zee," reflected Granfer, " and wanted zo much stick
as any on 'em. I've a smacked 'un mezelf,"
added Granfer, with great dignity and importance ; " ay, and I smacked 'un well, I
did ! " repeated Granfer, with relish.

" You was allays a good 'un to smack,
Granfer," observed his grandson, the clerk,
with tender reminiscences of Granfer's opera-
tion on his own person.

" Whatever I done, I went through wi' 't,"
returned the old man, complacently digesting
this tribute to his prowess. " Ay, I've a
smacked 'un mezelf, and I smacked 'un well,
I did," he repeated, with ever-growing importance.

" Come along home ! " said Stevens, who
was waiting to lock the lych-gate. " You

bain't old enough to bide in churchyard for good, Granfer."

"Ah! I bain't a-gwine underground this ten year yet," returned Granfer, shaking his head, and slowly rising from his tombstone in the blue moonlight, his breath showing smokelike on the keen air, and his wrinkled hands numbed doubly by age and the winter night. "I baint a-gwine yet," he muttered to himself; while the group broke up in slow, rustic fashion, and they all trudged off, Tom leading the way, erect and martial, airily swinging his little cane, and stepping with a firm, even stride; Jim rolling along with a wide, swaying gait, as if there were an earthquake, and the churchyard ground were heaving and surging around him; the rustics tramping heavily after, with a stolid, forceful step, as if the ground beneath them were a stubborn enemy, to be mastered only by continued blows; and soon the grey church stood silent and deserted in the frosty moonlight, till the clock in the belfry pealed out five mellow strokes above the quiet, unheeding dead.

At that hour Ben Lee was on the point of leaving his stables and going home to tea. Judkins and he were kindling their pipes at the harness-room fire, each with a face of sullen gloom.

"It wasn't so much what he said," observed Judkins; "'twas how he said it made them all cry. He seemed kind of heart-broken about it, as though somebody belonging to him, some friend like, had done wrong."

"Do you think he was thinking of my poor girl?" asked Ben, quickly; and Judkins nodded assent.

"He always had a kind heart, had Mr. Cyril, and he thought a deal of Alma," continued Lee; "lent her good books and that."

"There was one in the church as wasn't upset, and looked as quiet as a whetstone all through—that damned doctor!" said the young man, fiercely.

"Dr. Everard? You don't think, Charles—— ?"

"Haven't I seen him walking in the wood with her?" he interrupted, with imprecations. "Why did he come sneaking into your house, doctoring your wife last spring, day after day without fail, and always something to say to Alma afterwards in another room? Answer me that, Ben Lee!"

The man was half stunned. "I'd break every bone in his cursed body," he burst out, purple with passion, "if I thought that! And the good he done my wife, too, and I that blind!"

"Blind you were, Ben Lee, and blind was everybody else. But I watched. I've seen them shake hands at the gate, and she giving of him flowers, damn him! I've seen them in the wood there, standing together, and he showing of her things through that glass of his that makes things bigger than they ought to be. Wait till I catch him, Ben, that's all! And he sitting through that sermon, and everybody crying, and even Mr. Ingram blowing his nose; he sitting as scornful and cold as any devil. There's no conscience in the likes of him!"

"Charles," cried Ben, suddenly clutching

the young man's arm with a grip that
brought the blood to his face, "I'll kill
him ! "

Ben was purple, and quivering from head
to foot, and Judkins's passionate anger sank
within him at the sight.

"Hush, Ben, hush ! " he said ; "don't you
do nothing rash. Killing's murder, Ben.
And that will do her no good.   No, no ; I'll
thrash him, and you shall thrash him, and he
shall be brought to book, sure enough ; that's
only justice."

Poor Ben dashed away his pipe, covered
his face with his coat-cuff, and broke out
crying.

"Lord ha' mercy ! " cried the young groom,
crying himself.   "You do take on, Ben.
Come, come, cheer up, man.   Better days'll
come, and you may see her married and
happy yet.   Come on home, Ben, come."

And he drew him out into the solemn quiet
of the winter moonlight, and took him across
the park and the meadow, and wished him
good night at the door of his sorrowful home.

" And mind you, Ben, don't you be hard on her," he said at parting.

" If Ben comes across him," he muttered to himself, as he strolled moodily up and down the high-road, whence he could see the Temple white in the moonlight, with its one window faintly aglow, " he'll do for him. Ben's hot, and he'll do for him, as sure as eggs is eggs." Then he vowed to himself that he would wreak his own revenge first, and, if possible, save Ben from yielding to his passionate nature. " I'll track him down like a hound !" he muttered, striking fiercely at the frosted hedgerow with the light whip he carried.

Everard, in the mean time, was serenely happy in the drawing-room at Malbourne, unconscious that he had an enemy in the world, much less that men were scheming against his honour and his life. Nay, he did not even dream that he had so much as a detractor; he loved his fellows, and was at peace with mankind.

The family were gathered in the drawing-room in pleasant Sunday idleness, save Mr. Maitland, who was visiting a sick parishioner. Cyril and Marion were side by side on a remote sofa, dreamily happy in each other's presence ; Henry had mounted his microscope within reach of Mrs. Maitland, and was displaying its wonders in calm happiness for her and Lilian. Mark Antony, after careful and minute inspection of every detail of the strange apparatus, had decided that it was harmless, though frivolous, and expressed this decision by deep contented purrs and an adjournment to Cyril's knee, where he saw a prospect of long continuation and peace ; and Lennie and Winnie occupied the hearthrug, and divided their attention between the dogs and the microscope.

When Lilian bent over the tube, with the strong light of the lamp touching her animated face, and her dress rustling against him, Henry thought he had never been so happy in his life. Now and again some little unexpected incident, some glance or tone, revealed to him the delicious truth that they loved each other. No one else suspected that any change had come over the fraternal relations of a lifetime; they possessed this young happiness as a secret, sacred treasure, and feared the moment when it must be revealed to the world. Everard was loth to part even with the sweet anguish of doubt which crossed his heaven from time to time; it was so delightful to watch and question every word and glance and gesture of Lilian's, and play upon them a perpetual daisy game—"She loves me, she loves me not, she loves me." Some deep instinct told him that never in all his life would he again taste such happiness as this blessed dawn of love yielded him. As for Lilian, her manner took a little shyness occasionally in the strange fear which is the shadow of unspeakable joy.

Soon the domestic quiet was broken, but not troubled, by the irruption of Stanley and Lyster Garrett, the two sons of Northover, who liked to lounge away a Sunday evening at the Rectory, and there was much discussion of the entertainment to be given the next

night to the villagers; and then the Garrett
girls were brought across the park to assist
in the little parliament, and kept to share
the informal supper which was a Sunday
feature at Malbourne.

During supper a note arrived from Swaynestone, bidding Everard come to luncheon next
day to meet the great Professor Hamlyn,
who had seen some paper of Everard's in a
scientific journal, and expressed a wish to see
the writer. This was a great pleasure to
Everard, and a little responsive light in
Lilian's face told him that she realized what
making this man's acquaintance meant to
him.

"The luncheon was a great success,"
Everard observed, on his return to the Rectory
in the afternoon next day. "The great man
was most gracious; he did me the honour of
contradicting me nine times. Sir Lionel, in
his gentle way, was a little horrified at his
lion's roar, but saw that I was specially
honoured in being selected for the royal
beast's refection."

He went on to tell how the great writer, who lived in the neighbourhood, and was entertaining the professor, had been present, and had been less overbearing in manner and milder in language than usual. His hair had, however, evidently not been brushed. He was questioning Sir Lionel about Cyril's sermon, in which he was interested, since he had a slight acquaintance with the Maitlands, and had already detected Cyril's bright parts. He heard of the sermon through his brother, who had been taking a country stroll the previous afternoon, and had sauntered unnoticed into the church, just at the beginning of the sermon, and returned home with the intelligence that a young genius had arisen in the neighbourhood, with a voice, manner, and power unequalled in his experience.

Ingram Swaynestone, who had accompanied Everard back to Malbourne, wondered that Cyril should stare abstractedly at the fire during this recital, as if it had no interest for him, and made some remark to him expressive of his own personal appreciation of the sermon.

"My good fellow," returned Cyril, facing about, and speaking in his easy, genial fashion, "do you suppose that I don't know that I have the 'gift of the gab,' as Everard calls it ? I don't know that one need be proud of it, any more than of having one's nose placed in the middle of one's face, instead of all askew, as befalls some people ; and yet the devil is quite active enough in persuading me to be vain of it without my friends' assistance."

"It strikes me, Cyril," broke in Everard, "that you and the devil are on very confidential terms. I should have thought an innocent young parson like you the very last person the arch-enemy would select to hob-and-nob with."

"As if the Premier were to hold confidential chats with the late Nana Sahib," added Ingram, laughing.

Cyril flushed hotly, and then said, with a quietly dignified air, of which he was master when he wished to rebuke gently, "You are light-hearted, Henry; your spirits run away with you."

Upon which Everard could not resist retorting, with unabashed gravity, "I trust that yours will not run away with you, Cyril, since they are of such a questionable complexion."

"Come, you idle people," broke in Lilian; "it is time to go to the schoolroom. Are you going to be a waiter, Ingram? There is no compulsion, remember. Henry and the two Garretts are enlisted. Keppel Everard is our Ganymede; Marion and I are Hebes. In plain English, we serve the tea, and Keppel the beer."

"Since all the posts are filled, I will engage myself as general slavey," said the good-tempered Ingram, rising and following Lilian to the schoolroom, where a substantial meal was spread, and Mr. Maitland, with his curate, Mr. Marvyn, was already receiving his humble guests, who, unlike the guests of more fashionable entertainments, liked to arrive before instead of after the appointed hour, and in this case came long before all the candles were lighted, so that they depended chiefly on firelight for illumination.

Soon, however, the tables were full, men, women, and children sitting before a bounteous supply of roast beef and potatoes, while the air became oppressive with the scent of crushed evergreens and steaming food. Mr. Maitland and his curate had one table; Cyril and the Rev. George Everard presided at another; and the children's special board rejoiced in Lennie and Winnie as host and hostess.

Profound gravity prevailed, broken only by an occasional feminine titter or childish laugh, though it was evident, from the expression of Granfer's face when he came to the end of his first plate of beef, that he contemplated making a remark, probably of a jocular nature. All the mirth of the feast seemed to be concentrated in the faces of the Hebes and Ganymedes, who flew about the room with the greatest enjoyment, and took

care that neither plate nor cup was empty.
The two most assiduous waiters were Ingram
Swaynestone and Everard, both of whom
appeared to have the gift of ubiquity, and
carved with a recklessness and rapidity that
astonished all beholders. It was not until
the pudding was finished, and grace had been
sung by the choir, that some symptoms of
mirth and enjoyment began to break out
among the rustic revellers, and Mr. Maitland
laughed with his usual heartiness at Granfer's
annual joke, a fine antique one, with the
mellowness of fifty years upon it.

It was pleasant, while the tables were being
cleared, and the people were grouped about
the room, to see Cyril move among his old
friends, saying to each exactly the right
thing, in the manner exactly fitted to charm
each; going up to Tom Hale, and laying
his hand affectionately on his stalwart, red-
coated shoulder, and calling the pleased flush
into his face by the manner in which he
alluded to old times, especially the immortal
battle.

"I should be sorry to fight you now, Tom," he added; "or Jim either. It is well that my calling makes me a man of peace, while yours make you men of war."

"Yes, Mr. Cyril, it is all very well to be strong," replied Tom; "but what's that to a head-piece like yours?"

"They would rather have a smile from Cyril than a whole dinner from the rest of us," Everard observed to Lilian, as he paused a moment in his toilsome occupation of re-arranging the room. "Just look at George," he added, pointing to his reverend brother, who was standing disconsolate and dejected in the quietest corner he could find; "he is afraid that people are enjoying themselves. He would give his head to be allowed to improve the occasion."

"He implored my father to substitute hymns and clerical addresses for our frivolous little entertainment," replied Lilian. "He asked him how he would answer for having let slip such a precious opportunity of preaching the Gospel."

"Such a gospel—

> "'The dismal news I tell,
> How our friends are all embarking
> For the fiery port of hell.'

Poor old George! What a dreary phantasmagoria life must seem to him!"

"Happily, he doesn't really believe his creed. He asked Granfer just now if he knew that he was standing on the brink of the grave. Granfer replied, 'Ay, I've ben a-standing there this ninety year and more, and I bain't, zo to zay, tired on't yet.'"

Everard went up to his brother, and accosted him. "I hope there is nothing wrong, George," he said; "you look as if something had disagreed with you."

"Thank you, Henry," he replied, "my health is, under Providence, excellent; but I grieve for the souls of these poor creatures. I have ascertained for a fact that Maitland has caused beer and tobacco to be placed in a class-room for the men. Why, oh, why will he not lead them to the only true source of comfort?"

The diners were now joined by other guests of a higher grade: Farmer Long and his family; other farmers; a fresh contingent of Garretts; and last, though not by any means least, Sir Lionel Swaynestone and his two pretty daughters.

Thereupon the choir, assisted by amateurs, struck up, " My love is like a red, red rose," and the concert began. Wax executed a solo on the clarionet of such fearful difficulty that Everard trembled lest he should break a blood-vessel; and everybody, including Mrs. Wax, who coursed frantically after his rapid runs and 'flourishes on the piano, breathed an inward thanksgiving when he had finished. A piano duet between Miss Swaynestone and Miss Garrett followed, and was not the less tumultuously applauded because the superior swiftness of Miss Garrett's fingers landed her at the finish two bars ahead of Miss Swaynestone, who played on to the end with unruffled composure. Nobody had taken the slightest notice of any of these performances, save Wax's,

which alarmed the nervous; but now a
change took place.   Cyril led Lilian on to
the platform, and Marion's piano prelude
was drowned by the sound of heavy feet
plunging in from the smoking-room, and
everybody listened attentively for what was
a really delicate entertainment for the ear—
a vocal duet between the twins.   Even Sir
Lionel left his stately calm to encore the
simple melody, while Granfer did serious
damage to the school floor with his stick.   It
was not that the brother and sister sang with
unusual skill, or that their voices were re-
markably good, taken apart; the charm lay
in the peculiar sweetness of tone resulting
from the exact blending of the two.

Ingram Swaynestone grumbled in a good-
tempered way at having to read after this
performance, and though he read a bit of
Dickens with great spirit and humour, Everard
observed that the audience only listened and
applauded as a matter of duty.   Ethel Swaynestone was an accomplished singer, but her
voice failed to please the rustic ear; while the

choir glees and other amateur music were received as a matter of course. But when Cyril once more stood on the platform, and began in his rich, pure voice, " There was a sound of revelry by night," Everard was startled at the sudden hush of attention that fell on the audience, and surprised at the richness of harmony in the well-known stanzas. When Cyril repeated the line, " But hush! hark! a deep sound strikes like a rising knell!" the rustics started and looked over their shoulders in dismay, and one susceptible matron uttered a faint shriek. " Did ye not hear it?" continued the reciter, in such thrilling tones that Mrs. Stevens, meeting the light of Cyril's blue eyes, took the question personally, and replied wildly in the negative, to the general consternation. Having brought this to a conclusion in such a manner that his unlettered audience actually saw the ball-room scene, " the cheeks all pale," the " tremblings of distress," and actually heard the sounds of approaching doom break in upon the brilliant revelry, and witnessed the

hurried departure of the troops to the terrible
field destined to be fertilized with " red rain,"
Cyril paused, to let the tumultuous encores
subside ; and, at last, when silence ensued,
began with a plaintive sweetness, that was in
strong contrast to the dramatic force and fire
of the " Eve of Waterloo "—

> " ' I remember, I remember,
>   The house where I was born,
>   The little window where the sun
>   Came peeping in at morn.
>   He never came a wink too soon,
>   Or brought too long a day ;
>   But now——' "

Here Cyril paused, with a deep sigh.

> " ' I often wish the night
>   Had borne my breath away.' "

To Everard's intense surprise, he not only
saw tears all round him, but found a sensation
of intense sorrow and longing for the past
stealing over himself, while the pathos of
Cyril's voice seemed to break his heart. He
saw, as they all saw, Malbourne Rectory, and
Cyril, a boy once more—gentle, happy, and

full of sweet, innocent fancies; and when the latter went on, in his quiet voice, so full of melodious heart-break—

> "'And where my brother set
> The laburnum on his birthday:
> That tree is living yet,'"

something rushed up into Everard's throat and half choked him. He knew that Cyril was thinking of a rose-tree he had planted on a far-off birthday.

> "'But now 'tis little joy,'"

said Cyril, with a voice full of tears—

> "'To know I'm farther off from heaven
> Than when I was a boy.'"

There was no applause to this; complete and tearful silence reigned when he finished and stepped quietly down among his friends, where Sir Lionel gently rebuked him for playing so cruelly on their feelings, and added; "As I said to Ingram yesterday, such a voice and manner would sway the House;" and every one was relieved when the choir struck up, "All among the Barley."

Lilian was among the few who did not give way to tears during the recital of Hood's pathetic little poem, though Everard, who hovered near her all the evening, observed that her large, soft grey eyes were dewy wet, as was their wont when she was moved, and her face reflected all the changes on her brother's. It was not easy to get very close to Lilian, because she was fenced in, as it were, by a little ring of children, who clung to her skirts, and laid their cheeks against her beautiful, slender hands, and were perfectly happy with the privilege of touching her.

"I do not think," she said, while returning to the Rectory through the frosty moonlight with Everard, "that Cyril is farther off from heaven than when he was a boy. Indeed, it seems to me that one must grow nearer to it with every day of life, unless one deliberately turns from it."

"You are speaking from your own experience," replied Henry. "Men are different. To go through early manhood is to be drawn over a morass of temptation, into which, with

the best intentions, most men sink occasionally."

"Not men like Cyril, Henry. He is so
slightly weighted with flesh that he would
skim dry-footed over the most quaking quag-
mire. I know every thought in Cyril's
heart."

Everard was half inclined to endorse this
opinion of Cyril. He recognized in his
friend's character a certain feminine element,
that *ewig weibliche* which Goethe pronounces
the saving ingredient in human nature. The
protecting tenderness with which he loved
the bright, gentle boy, two years his junior
and less robust than himself, still lived in his
deep affection for the pious and intellectual
young priest. Cyril's feelings were sacred to
him as a woman's; he feared to sully their
delicate bloom by harsh allusions to the bare
facts of life. He was one of the twins, both
of whom were objects of his lifelong tenderness. And Cyril had his moods, like a woman
—a peculiarity not without fascination for
Everard's more thoroughly masculine mind.

A soft mood was on Cyril that night. He knocked at Everard's door after every one had retired for the night, and drew a chair to his side by the fire, before which the doctor was smoking, and, investing himself in one of Everard's coats, lighted a pipe of his own.

"The coolness with which the fellow takes my coats!" growled Everard.

"It is no matter if your coats smell of tobacco," replied Cyril, tranquilly; "I smoke so seldom that I have no smoking-coats. To-night I am restless."

"Why so pale and wan, fond lover?" laughed Everard. "Because Marion is gone back to Woodlands for two days, I suppose."

"You may laugh, Henry, but I feel more than lost without her. I am helpless, separated from the best influence of my life."

"You are a slave to your feelings; learn to master them."

"It is true," replied Cyril. "You are the best and wisest friend ever man had. I never regretted doing anything you advised. I shall always be grateful to you for making me read up for mathematical honours. I needed that discipline to steady me. I have never valued you as you deserve; only now and again it flashes upon me that what I take for granted is of superior worth. How selfish I was about letting Marion join you in the Mediterranean! You little dream how I suffered for that. Well, without you, Marion and I would have been parted for ever."

" Without Lilian."

" You and Lilian together. How selfish and weak I was! and the harm that came from it ! "

" Oh, come! It's all right now; a forgotten story.

" There are things that can never be forgotten," sighed Cyril, with the pathetic intonation that had broken people's hearts in the evening. " To give way to a sin, only one sin, is like letting a little water through a dyke. A child may begin it, but once begun, the terrible consequences sweep endlessly on, a very flood of iniquity. I suppose there is nothing which has the power of multiplying itself like sin. One hideous consequence begets a hundred more hideous," continued Cyril, staring moodily at the fire, while his pipe lay extinct and neglected by his side.

" I see no pulpit, your reverence," said Everard, who was puffing away with quiet enjoyment.

Cyril turned with one of his sudden changes, and flashed a mirthful glance of his strange blue eyes on his friend, and, replenishing his pipe from the tobacco which Keppel had brought for Everard on his return from his last voyage, broke into a strain of gay affectionate chat, full of a thousand reminiscences of the school-days they passed together under Mr. Marvyn's care in the quiet village.

" What a fellow you were!" exclaimed Cyril, with enthusiasm, after recalling a certain story of a Sèvres vase; and, though Everard only grunted, he looked at the graceful, animated figure before him with an affectionate adoration that made him feel it would be a pleasure to die for such a man. " I was afraid when I smashed the vase," continued Cyril, "and but for you should have hidden it. I never shall forget seeing you walk up to Lady Swaynestone and tell her that we had run up against the vase and broken it. I felt such a sneak; I had done it, and you took the blame on yourself, and got the punishment. She said no word, but delivered you such a box on the ear as made mine tingle, and sent you staggering across the room. Then her anger found words, and you bore it all."

"I never knew a ruder or more ill-bred woman," said Everard.

"I suppose you got over the box on the ear in an hour or two," continued Cyril; "but I did not. I was miserable for days, hating myself, and yet too frightened to tell the truth."

Everard here produced a yawn of cavernous intensity, and dropped his pipe in sheer drowsiness; but Maitland seemed more alert than ever, and rose in his restlessness and looked out of the window on the dark vault of shimmering stars.

"The night wanes," he said; "one day more, and the weary old year will be done—only one day."

"Ungrateful fellow!" said Everard, stretching himself till he seemed gigantic; "such a good old year. I shall be sorry to say good-bye to him, for my part."

Cyril dropped the curtain and turned to the fire, his features all alight. "Let us look forward," he said, "to the rosy future. Welcome to sixty-three, Harry; it is full of promise for us both! Good night, dear lad, and God bless you!"

And, with a warm hand-clasp, he took his leave, but turned again, lingering, irresolute; and then, with another warm hand-clasp and blessing, left his drowsy friend to his slumbers, just as the church clock was striking three.

CHAPTER IX.

THE last day of the year dawned bright and cloudless, a very prince and pearl of winter days, and Everard's heart bounded within him as he looked out on the ruddy morning, and felt it a joy merely to live.

"I shall long remember sixty-two," he thought; "it has been a good year, and to-day will crown and complete the whole. To-day I will make sure of my fate."

The wine of life never before had the sparkle and effervescence of that morning; it was almost too much for a sober mind. Had Everard been superstitious, or even introspective, he would have presaged disaster at hand. Instead of which, he rejoiced in his youth, and felt as if his body were turned to air, as he sprang down the staircase and into the sunny breakfast-room.

Mr. Maitland was late that morning, and Cyril read the simple household prayers. Everard loved this sweet custom of family prayer, remiss as he often was in assisting personally at it; it seemed so fit and harmonious for that holy incense to ascend from the altar of the innocent country home, and to-day it acquired a sort of pathos from the youth and grace of the reader. The scene lived long in his mind, irradiated by a sweet light of peace and holiness : the kneeling children and Lilian, the sunshine touching their hair; the bowed heads of the maids; the dignified bearing of the reader; the music of his voice—a voice soft now, and soothing as the murmur of the brook beneath the trees, with none of the tragic tones they knew so well. Just as Cyril was about to pronounce the closing benediction, Mr. Maitland, thinking the prayers done, entered, and, seeing how they were employed, dropped on his knees in time to receive the lad's blessing.

The sight of that grey head, bent thus before the young priest's benison, touched Everard profoundly, and he felt humbled to think of his own world-stained soul by the side of these spotless creatures—priests and women and children.

"Lead us not into temptation," said Cyril's pure, rich voice, chorused by the innocent trebles and Everard's own faltering bass.

What temptation could possibly befall those guileless beings that day? What harsh dissonance could ever mar the music of those tuneful lives? he wondered. And he was glad that his own faltering petition had gone up to Heaven with those of hearts so pure, though even he could scarcely fall into temptation in that sweet spot, he thought.

Cyril announced his intention of walking into Oldport that bright morning, and Lilian, of course, was to go part of the way with him. Everard had been asked to shoot over some of the Swaynestone covers, and rather surprised Cyril, who knew that his friend liked sport, by saying that he had declined the shooting-party, and wanted to join the pedestrians.

"You had far better shoot, Henry," he said; "a mere walk is a stupid thing for you. You have had no amusement whatever since you have been here."

"To-morrow we plunge into a vortex of dissipation," said Everard. "Will you give me the first dance, Lilian? By the way, I suppose his reverence has given up these frivolities."

"Oh, I shall dance at Woodlands to-morrow," replied Cyril. "Just two square dances with Marion, and then, I suppose, farewell to such delights."

"I cannot say that I like to see a clergy-man dancing," observed his father, "though I danced myself till I was forty, and should enjoy a turn with the young people even now."

"Then, let us have a quiet carpet-dance while the boys are here," said Lilian; "just the Swaynestones and Garretts and Marion, and father shall dance with each of us in turn."

"Oh yes!" cried Everard; and Cyril chimed

in with great animation, "Just one more fling for me;" and Mr. Maitland went off laughing, and saying he had nothing to do with it—they must ask their mother, and Lennie and Winnie jumped for joy, and announced that they should not go to bed before their elders, and the little *fête* was regarded as a pleasant certainty.

Cyril kept them waiting some minutes after the appointed time for starting. He had important letters to write, he said; and when at last he appeared, his face was full of care and perplexity. In the mean time, Lilian and Everard were very happy on the sunny lawn together, visiting the invalid donkey and other animals, and wandering about their old playground, past the spot where the twins used to play at Robinson Crusoe, and where Everard helped them build a hut, and recalling a thousand pleasant memories of their childish labours and sports. There was hoarfrost on the delicate branches of the leafless trees, and the sunshine was broken into a thousand jewel-like radiances by the little sharp facets of the ice-crystals. There was an unwonted sparkle also in Lilian's eyes, and a deeper glow on her cheeks than usual. The air was like wine.

· The blacksmith was clinking merrily at his glowing forge as they passed along the road, and his blithe music carried far in the still air. Granfer was sunning himself outside, according to custom, ready for a chat with anybody, and commanding from his position a view of all the approaches to the village. Hale, the wheelwright, was there, getting some ironwork done, and turned with Granfer to look after the trio.

"Ay," observed the latter, shaking his head wisely, "a viner pair than they twins o' ourn you never see, John Hale, so well matched they be as Sir Lionel's bays."

"A pretty pair," replied the wheelwright; "but give me the doctor. There's muscle and build!"

"Ay," echoed Straun, between the rhythmic hammer-strokes; "a man like he's a credit to his vittles."

The young doctor's appearance certainly justified this observation, and his walk and bearing fully set off the robust manliness of his athletic frame, which was further enhanced by contrast with Cyril's slender grace. The friends were of similar height, but Henry's shoulders were higher, and made him look taller; his chest and back were far broader than Cyril's, and his well-balanced limbs were hard with muscle. The suit of grey which he wore gave him breadth, and displayed his form more fully than did Cyril's black broadcloth of severe clerical cut, which had, moreover, the well-known effect of lessening the outlines of the figure. The delicate glow which the sparkling air had called into Cyril's worn cheek was very different from the firm hue of health in Henry's honest face; and the fearless, frank gaze of his bright brown eyes, and the light brown moustache, looking golden in the sunshine, gave him an older look than Cyril's clean-shaven features wore.

Hale observed to Granfer that whoever

attacked the doctor on a dark night would
find him an ugly customer, which Granfer
admitted, adding that Cyril's strength all went
to brain-power, in which he was supreme.
Lilian also observed Henry's athletic appearance in contrast with her brother's slight
build, and then she remembered how the
friends but the day before had been playing
with the children in the hall, and the fragile-
looking Cyril had given his muscular friend
a blow so clean and straight and well-planted
that the doctor had gone down like a ninepin
before it, to the great amusement of the
children and satisfaction of Everard.

Farmer Long was driving into Oldport in
his gig, and there beside him sat Mr. Marvyn,
charmed to see his three pupils together.
" I shall not see you again, Henry," he said
regretfully, " unless you stay over Sunday.
I only came back for the entertainment
yesterday. I have a parson's week to finish.
Cyril I shall see again." And so they parted
with regret, since Everard was greatly
attached to his old tutor, who had encouraged

and developed his taste for natural science,
and upheld him in his choice of a profession.
" And I wanted to tell old Marvyn about my
germ theory," Everard said, as the gig disappeared.

" You will be able to tell the whole world
soon," replied Lilian, to whom the theory
had been confided and explained that very
morning.

" Not yet," said Everard ; " it takes years
of patient study and experiment to verify a
scientific theory."

" Old Hal always was a patient fellow,"
Cyril observed. " Do you remember the rows
about his dissections in his bedroom, Lill ? "

Lilian replied that she remembered the
odours, and they all laughed over the old
schoolroom jokes and catastrophes, and were
very happy as they climbed the hillside by
a field-path, leaving the road below them.
Afterwards Everard remembered the rare and
affectionate expression, " Old Hal." And now
in the bright sunshine he was pleased to see
Cyril so like his old self, careless, cordial,

and light-hearted, all the asceticism and sadness put away ; ambition, toil, and care completely forgotten. He knew that Cyril loved
Marion truly, and would be happy with her,
and yet it struck him that morning that his
strong, half-instinctive affection for his twin
sister touched a yet deeper chord in his
nature. Now that Marion was away, there
was a greater ease about the twins ; each
seemed to develop the other's thoughts in
some mysterious manner. They laughed to
each other, and walked hand-in-hand like
children, seeing everything through each
other's eyes—the still, sunny winter fields
and brown woods stretching away to the sea,
the flocks of weird white sea-gulls, the occasional rabbit or pheasant starting up before
them, the larks, silent now, fluttering over
the grassy furrows, the bright berries in
copse and hedgerow, the sheep peacefully
munching the mangolds a solitary shepherd
was cutting for them in a lonely field. They
called each other Cyll and Lill, abbreviations
none else ever used ; they contradicted each

other as they never dreamed of contradicting
anybody else.

Everard walked along, sometimes by their
side, sometimes behind them, as the nature
of the path obliged, and listened to them
and loved them. The twins were never so
delicious to him as when together in his
familiar presence, of which they seemed to
make no account. So long as those two
could meet together thus, an immortal childhood would be theirs, he thought; age could
never rob the beautiful bond between them
of its bloom. Presently they quarrelled.
Lilian sat on a felled tree in the woods
through which they were passing; Cyril
leant up against a tree; and Everard looked
on with amusement, and loved them all the
more in their childishness.

"Oh, you babes in the wood!" he cried
at last; whereupon Cyril flashed upon him
one of his droll glances, and laughed.

"Come, Lill," he said, "I forgive you this
time."

Absolute harmony and utter unconsciousness of past anger was established between them on the instant, and Everard was amused to hear them plunge straightway into a grave discussion upon the limits of free-will.

They were now high on the crest of the hill, and could see the lovely stretches of down sweeping away to the unseen sea on one side, while on the other the Swaynestone lands sloped down with wood and park and farmstead till they merged in the horizon, which was broken here and there by tiny blue bays of inland sea on the north.

There was no sound; all the song-birds, even the robin, were hushed by the frost, and the whole landscape lay silent before them, folded in the awful purity of winter sunshine. The shadows in the hills and woods were blue, and distant objects looked immensely far in the violet haze of the winter morning. Here they paused, deep in their argument, and looked down over the tranquil woods and saw the white front of Swaynestone House gleaming in the sun.

Down in a low-lying fallow field there were some black specks motionless in the furrows; suddenly they rose in a black cloud of wings, and there were a hundred silver flashes against the belt of coppice bordering the field. Higher still the cloud rose, and swift gleams of black and silver flashed in rhythmic sequence against the pure blue of the sky, and the weird wail of the plover was heard faintly, as the flock floated in a dazzle of white bodies and black wings over the coppice till they reached another field, into the furrows of which they dropped motionless. While Everard and Lilian were watching the plovers, they did not observe that Cyril plunged into the wood behind them and put his hand into the hollow of a tree.

"I was looking for a squirrel's nest," he said, strolling back again. "Listen; I will imitate a chaffinch."

It was a trick they used to practice when parted from each other in the woods, and they looked down over the roof of the

Temple, which lay among the trees below them, and thought of their old rambles for nuts and blackberries, when little Alma would often join them and tell them where to find heavy-laden boughs and brambles. Suddenly from among the trees rose the call of another chaffinch, exactly corresponding to Cyril's.

"Some children at play," said Cyril, carelessly; "Lennie and Winnie, perhaps. They were going to Swaynestone to slide. I must get on, Everard; I have a lot to do in Oldport."

"'Jog on, jog on, the footpath way,
    And merrily hent the stile-a :
    A merry heart goes all the day,
    Your sad tires in a mile-a,'"

Everard sang out in his deep voice, as the trio continued their walk at a mended pace.

After another mile through hanging woods of beech and sycamore, they descended a hill and climbed another crested with coppice, through which they passed, brushing the heavy hoar-frost from the dead leaves and twigs as they went, and pausing for Lilian to show them the haunt of a little wren in a bank. The tiny bird, attracted by some crumbs sprinkled on her muff, came cautiously out, climbed up her arm, pecked its dainty meal, and suffered itself to be raised on the muff to the level of her face, in which it gazed confidingly, even venturing to peck at a little stray fluff of a curl which stole over her neck. Everard and Maitland stood apart and watched this pleasant comedy.

"You had the same power over animals as Lilian," Everard observed to Cyril. "What is its secret, I wonder?"

"There are three moral factors," replied Cyril: "perfect self-control, that warm and intelligent affection which we call sympathy, and innocence. Lilian is the most guileless human being on the face of this earth. There must also be some physical attraction, I suspect—some mesmeric or electric power, of which we know little."

"But surely you possess the three moral factors; how is it you have lost your power? Lilian was saying only last night that the good draw nearer heaven with increasing years, and you, whose life has been not merely stainless, but austere——"

"Henry," interrupted Cyril, in his most pathetic voice, "I am a *man!*"

Lilian had replaced her tiny friend at its house-door, and now joined the young men, who went on their way, Everard struck and startled by the heart-broken accent Cyril laid on the word *man,* and wondering if the morbid tone he had of late detected in the young priest's mind did not almost verge on insanity.

At the end of the coppice through which they were passing was a stile standing on a steep bank, which led by rough steps down into the high-road, and here they parted, the twins once more falling into discord, each offering Henry as a companion to the other, and declining to selfishly appropriate him, until he laughingly suggested that he was no mere chattel, but a being endowed with will; also that his will decided to take the homeward path with Lilian—a decision which evidently satisfied Cyril, who sprang down the steep bank, and turned, on reaching the road, to the stile—over which the other two leaned—with a laughing face, and lifted his hat in his own graceful manner. They gazed after the light, well-carried figure for a moment or two, little imagining how all the light died out of the bright young face when it turned from them, what a weight of trouble lined the clear brow and drew down the corners of the delicate mouth, and added ten years, at least, to his apparent age, and then they began to retrace their steps through the wood.

"It is like old times," Lilian observed. "Cyril and I are growing old and wise, Henry; we are seldom like that now. We seem to grow apart, which we must expect."

" 'The old order changeth, giving place to new,' " quoted Everard. "The new may be better, but one does not like to part with the old," he added falteringly, after a pause.

"The old—was good," replied Lilian, rather absently; and the perfect self-command of which her brother had spoken suddenly deserted her, with the consciousness that the story of her life and love was approaching a crisis, and the two walked on in silence.

Everard's bright spirits seemed to have flown onwards in the wake of Cyril, his heart sank down like a thing of lead, and a dreadful vision of all his sins and shortcomings, his weaknesses and failings, rose ghastly and oppressive before him. Henry Everard appeared to him as the merest rag of a man— the most complete failure that ever issued from the workshops of nature and education. He stole a glance at Lilian, walking with her light step and airy carriage by his side; a sweet picture of stainless womanhood, her cheek flushed with purest rose by exercise, her eyes cast down contrary to their wont, her hair touched into golden tints by the sunlight, and the outline of her form traced clearly against a background of frosted hazel boughs, and his spirit died within him. What had he to offer her? How could he ever dare? And yet—— Lilian turned under the stress of his ardent gaze, and met his eyes for one swift moment; then her looks resumed their commerce with the mossy, frost-veined path, and a rich rush of crimson flooded her face.

"Lilian," began Henry, breathlessly, "we have been great friends all our lives."

"Yes," replied Lilian, regaining her natural mental poise; "Cyril and I always appropriate each other's goods."

"Supposing Cyril out of the question." he added hastily, "would you not care for—value my friendship? In short, am I not your own personal friend? Don't you care a little for me for my own sake, Lilian?"

"Indeed I do, dear Henry," she replied, a little tremulously. "There is no friend for whom I—whom I value more highly. That is—yes, we are real friends."

"You were always dear to me, very dear—as dear as Marion herself," continued Henry; "but you have become the dearest of all since I scarcely know when—the very dearest human being on earth. Oh, Lilian, the truth is that I love you with all my heart! I have loved you long; I cannot tell when I began."

"That is not the important question," returned Lilian, with a little smile dawning about her lips and eyes. "The question is, how long do you mean to go on?"

The same quaint, half-humorous, half-pathetic expression which so often lighted Cyril's pale blue eyes now gleamed from Lilian's gray orbs, moistened with the sweet dew which so frequently enhanced their lustre, and even in that passionate moment Henry observed this, and thought how closely his love and his friendship were bound together, and realized that Cyril was dearer than ever to him now that Lilian was his.

The answer to Lilian's playful earnest was the old immemorial assertion of lovers, repeated with endless delightful iteration, long drawn out with Heaven knows how much unnecessary sweetness. The old unvarying song the birds sing every spring, with a fresh charm that never cloys, though the white-headed man heard it in his childhood, and in the days when he too swelled the many-voiced marriage hymn which ascends perpetually from the youth and strength of earth; the old eternal song which is yet the freshest sound that ever falls on the ear of youth, and fills it with a sweet bewildered surprise ;· the theme which changed Eden from a prison to a home ;—this delicious melody was sung over again in the wintry woods that day, when all the birds were hushed by the frost, and the earth lay still in its winter trance.

The singing of this pleasant duet took a long time, and the low midwinter sun passed its meridian and travelled some distance on its westward way, while they strolled slowly on with many pauses, slowly enough to chill blood not warmed by the current of vital flame which young Love sends through the veins, until they reached the spot above the Temple, where they watched the plovers' flight in the morning. They paused there.

At that moment a delicate music floated up from the valley, the well-known, cheery chiming of the waggon-bells. Nearer and nearer the golden harmony swelled, stronger and stronger the fairy peals waxed, as the team approached on its way along the high-road to Oldport, till the soft chimes came tumbling in the full power of their sweet turbulence upon the clear, still air.

"Those are our wedding-bells," said Everard, as they passed on and let the melodious clashing die away behind them in the distance. "It is a good omen."

CHAPTER X.

THE irony of fate will often have it so that when life gains its culminating point of happiness, it is but one degree from the darkest hour of overthrow; just as the blossom has reached its sweetest bloom, the blighting frost comes, and all is over. When Everard and Lilian exchanged the promise whose sweetness was to live through so many dark and lonely years, they little dreamed that any peril was near them in the silent wood. They saw no crouching figure trembling behind the hazel bushes; they did not guess that any eye, save those of the wild creatures of the wood, witnessed their betrothal; and they went on their way rejoicing, making plans for the happy future they were to spend side by side.

When Ben Lee went home to dinner that day, the young groom, Judkins, accompanied him, as he often did now, finding a strange solace to his own grief in that of the troubled father, and pleased that the old man turned to him for consolation. He usually left Lee at the door, but on this occasion Mrs. Lee came out and beckoned him in.

"She's gone to meet him," she said excitedly. "She made believe to go and gather a bit of brushwood in the garden, and she's off up the hill to the wood. He must have passed an hour ago, and there was the whistle of a chaffinch for signal. I heard her whistle back, the deceitful faggot, though she thought I was safe out of the way, and she's been watching for an opportunity ever since. Straight up the hill she went, Lee, not twenty minutes gone."

While Mrs. Lee was speaking, the two men had followed her through the house, and now stood in the back garden, whence they could see the whole slope of the hill, with its woody crest traced clear against the blue

midday sky. Beneath this crest the trees
had been cleared in a straight, broad strip
about the breadth of the little garden.

"Look here, Ben!" cried Judkins, seizing
the arm of Lee, who was striding rapidly
through the garden, and was about to ascend
the treeless slope; "don't you do nothing
rash, now."

Lee's face was purple, and he shook the
younger man off with a muttered oath, when
the latter once more caught him by the arm,
and pointed upwards, with a cry.

"I knew it; I always knew it. The damned
scoundrel!"

Just within the shadow of the wood, which
partly screened them, were two figures, the
inner and less seen, that of a woman in dark
winter clothing; the outer, that of a man in
a suit of grey. The light hazel twigs im-
pinged but slightly on the latter figure, so
that its outline was distinctly seen, and the
face itself was even visible sideways for a
moment. The female figure, on the contrary,
with the face hidden in the other's arm, and

its dark outlines less striking by their colour, could only be guessed at. The vision lasted but a moment; the figures moved on over the woodland path. The hazels were denser there, and the path turned into the wood, so that the pair were gradually hidden, and soon completely vanished from sight.

"I'm witness, mind," Judkins muttered, while Lee groaned aloud. "You and me saw him go through the village this morning in those grey clothes and that hat."

So saying, the young man turned and went rapidly back, avoiding the garden, and plunging into the shadow of the trees which bordered it on either side, while Lee toiled up the hill. He had not gone far before Alma appeared at the spot where the hazels grew thin, and issued from the wood. She started slightly when she saw her father, but soon regained her composure, and advanced towards him.

"What were you doing in the wood?" he asked harshly.

"I only went up for a little fresh air this fine day," she replied gently.

" Went up to hear the birds sing, perhaps,"
he continued, with savage sarcasm.

" There are no birds singing now," said
Alma, sadly. " Even the robin is silent in
the frost."

" Ay, and the chaffinch. Who were you
speaking to a minute ago ? "

" Nobody," she replied, looking surprised.

" That's a damned lie, Alma ! "

" I have spoken to no human being but
you and mother this week past," said Alma,
in a tone of weary apathy.

They had reached the garden now, and
Alma went in, scarcely hearing the impreca-
tion that burst from her maddened father's
lips.

Lee remained behind her ; then re-ascended
the hill and picked up a little scrap of paper
he had seen Alma tear in halves and drop
when she thought herself unobserved. He
pieced it together, and read, written in a
disguised, backward-slanting hand, " At dusk
to-night. The old spot. Important."

" Oh, Alma ! " he cried ; " my pretty

Alma! my only child!" Then he turned back, his brow darkening as he went, till the momentary tenderness was quite effaced, and he muttered fiercely beneath his breath, " I'll kill him! I'll kill him!"

It was late when the unconscious lovers reached home. The bell was ringing for luncheon, and Mark Antony was sitting on the doorstep, looking very cross at his mistress's delay; for he was a cat of regular habits, and particularly disliked waiting for meals. He received Lilian rather distantly, accepted Henry's caress with haughty disdain, and then boxed Snip's ears for barking inopportunely.

"Oh, I say, Henry!" cried Lennie, who was bounding into the dining-room with fresh-brushed hair and clean collar, "ain't you in a mess?"

Henry had slipped on a damp bank by a stream, in trying to gather some ivy coloured crimson and gold for Lilian, and a great brown-and-green stain showed strikingly on the knee of his grey suit. In two bounds he was in his room, and in three seconds out of the stained suit and into another, consisting of a black coat and lower garments of the same tone of grey as those discarded. The grey suit was folded neatly and placed on a chair; and he appeared at the table in less than five minutes in that perfect neatness and cleanliness which so especially distinguish the English gentleman.

No one observed his change of dress, though everybody had noticed the morning's grey suit. It was rather light in colour for the season, according to the fashion of that day, and had commended itself to Everard from the sense of cleanliness that light colours always afforded him. Lilian, indeed, observed that the grey coat was replaced by a black one, and, in speculating afterwards on the subject, she came to the conclusion that the black had probably been assumed for indoor wear, as being cooler than the thick frieze.

Marion appeared at luncheon, having dropped in on her way to Oldport, where she had errands in connection with the New

Year's ball at Woodlands. She made a charming little face of disappointment at the non-appearance of Cyril; but the disappointment by no means spoilt her appetite, and she kept them all alive by her sprightly conversation and playful, endearing ways. She petted Mr. Maitland in a most enchanting manner; teased the children and the cat; was impertinent to Lilian when gently rebuked for these misdemeanours; snubbed her brother, according to her usual custom; and was very tender in the little cares she lavished on Mrs. Maitland. Her vivacity, and the bright, warm-coloured style of her beauty, and the aërial lightness of her form made a good foil to Lilian's repose and gentle dignity, the quieter tones of her colouring, and the more majestic development of her figure.

Everard regarded his sister as a charming wayward child, loved her little rebellious ways, and put up contentedly with all her naughtiness. He was six years her senior, and had been the youngest of the family till her birth, which cost their mother her life; and then the orphan baby became the object of his tenderest care, and he soothed away his own sorrowful sense of orphanhood by hovering over the tiny sister's slumbers, and amusing her waking moments by all kinds of childish devices. It was partly for the baby's sake that he was never sent to school; partly also in obedience to the request of his dead mother, who judged, from her experience of the elder boys, that the benefits of public schools were overbalanced by their contaminations and temptations. All his life he had been Marion's devoted slave, and, like other despots, she received his devotion with a satisfaction not unmingled with contempt.

" What on earth is Cyril doing in Oldport all day ? " Marion asked. " What business can he possibly have ? "

" Upon my word, I cannot imagine," replied Mr. Maitland, who had not considered the subject before.

And Marion's question set Everard thinking. Cyril was not likely to make many purchases in the little country town; his affairs were in the hands of London lawyers; he could not want money; he had no friends there; in short, it was very odd that he should spend the day in a little market town on business that could not be postponed, and so miss the partly expected visit of Marion.

Marion, however, carried Mr. Maitland off with her after luncheon, on his remembering that he had certain commissions to execute, and Lilian drove to Swaynestone to pay her long-promised call on Lady Swaynestone, and advise her about her charities according to her request. She had a thousand things to do, and was much troubled that she could not visit a certain Widow Dove, who lived in a lonely cottage on the down, that afternoon, and carry her a little present of money. So Henry, finding that he could not be allowed to accompany Lilian to Lady Swaynestone's, since the ladies wished to discuss business, offered to be Lilian's almoner, and was eagerly accepted.

He saw Lilian and the children off in the

pony-carriage, and then betook himself to
writing some letters in the room called
Lilian's; and, having done this, he remembered that Lilian had lamented having
no time to frame and hang the photograph
of Guercino's picture, and did this for her,
the frame having been already furnished by
the village carpenter.

In the mean time, at about three o'clock,
Cyril appeared in the drawing-room, where
Mrs. Maitland was lying on her couch. He
had finished his business, got some luncheon
at Oldport, and been picked up just out of
the town by Farmer Long, who drove him
home in his gig, he said. Then, after ten
minutes' chat with his mother, he went to his
room, telling her that he wished to get a
sermon ready for the next Sunday, when he
was to be at work again, and requesting that
he might not be disturbed till dinner.

All this Mrs. Maitland told Everard, when
he looked into the drawing-room a few
minutes later.

"I begged him to put off his sermon-

writing till another day," she said, " for he
looked woefully haggard and weary ; but I
could not persuade him.   He says he feels so
burdened until he has got his Sunday's
sermons off his mind.   Just like his father.
He always does his sermons on Monday, if
he can, and feels a free man for the rest of
the week."

" It is rather odd," Everard observed,
" that Cyril should spend so much time in
writing his sermons ; for he is supposed to
be an extempore preacher."

" Last Sunday's sermon was certainly
extempore," his mother replied ; " he had
some manuscript, but scarcely referred to it
more than once.   I wonder if I am a very
foolish old woman, Henry, for thinking that
Cyril has a really singular gift in preaching ?
His voice appears to me to be something
quite out of the common.   And I have heard
John Bright's oratory, and Gladstone's, and
D'Israeli's, the best preachers in our own
Church, and those brilliant Roman Catholics
who attracted such crowds to Notre Dame."

"I think, Mrs. Maitland," replied Everard, who was rather distraught in his manner, since he was nerving himself to introduce the topic of his engagement, "that Cyril will be reckoned the greatest preacher in the Church of England."

Then some people called, and Everard made his escape as soon as he decently could, and at about a quarter to four he started on his walk to Widow Dove's with a light heart. His road was, as far as the wood above the Temple, the same as that he had pursued so happily with Lilian an hour or two before, and it filled him with unspeakable rapture to recall the delightful incidents in his morning walk as he went, so that he was dreamy and unobservant, and scarcely spoke to the people he met on his solitary ramble, a thing very unusual with him.

The sun was declining redly and with great pomp of cloud scenery in the west—a glorious ending, he thought, of the happiest of happy years; and that was the only clue he had to the time of his starting, when referring in memory to this fatal walk, since he omitted, in his dreamy abstraction, to look at his watch, though he was naturally so precise in his habits, and had such a keen sense of the passage of time.

When he reached Widow Dove's lonely dwelling, he found it cold and dark, the door shut, and no smoke issuing from the chimney; the widow and her daughter were evidently gone away for a day or two. He felt a sort of eerie shiver at the darkness and gloom of the solitary homestead, though he little dreamt that his fate or the fate of those he loved could be influenced by a circumstance so trifling as the emptiness of a secluded cottage.

Then he turned his face homewards in the gathering dusk, choosing another way from that by which he came, by that strange fatality which pursues doomed men, and strode gaily and swiftly along over the open down, every dimple and hollow of which were familiar to him from boyhood. Some stars were out now, sparkling keenly in the

clear, frosty sky, in which the moon had not
yet risen. Over hedge and ditch, and through
copses, and round plantations Everard sped
blithely, until he approached the high-road
leading to Malbourne. Here his pace slackened, and he listened carefully for the sound
of Long's waggon-bells, which he thought
would carry far in the frosty stillness.

But there was no repetition of the fairy
peals which rang so blithely in the morning,
and he got as far as the wheelwright's
corner without having heard them. Grove,
the waggoner, was to bring him a parcel
from Oldport, a little parcel that he feared
might be forgotten if he did not intercept it.
Here he met Granfer, toiling slowly along
on his way to spend the evening at Hale's,
whose wife was one of his numerous de-
scendants. Had Granfer heard the team go
by? he asked.

"No, I ain't a yeard 'em since this
marning, zo to zay; not as I knows on,
Dr. Everard," Granfer replied, with his usual
circumlocution. "I 'lows I yeared 'em's

marning, zure enough. They was a-gwine into Oldport, as I hreckons, as you med zay zumwheres about noon or thereabouts. No, I 'lows I ain't a-yeared nor a bell zince that there; not as I knows on, I ain't."

After some further conversation, Everard strolled slowly on in the direction of Long's farm, full of anxiety about his precious packet, which he knew would fade. Near Long's he heard that the team had returned some time before, and his packet had been sent to the Rectory.

Striking across the fields, he returned in the deepening night, without going through the village, and, meeting with a little delay in consequence of an old gap having been recently stopped in a fence—a good stiff bullfinch—he gained the Rectory at about six o'clock, thus missing, to his disgust, the charmed hour of tea. There, when he entered, was the precious little box on the hall table, and he caught it up, and was going to unfasten it in his room, when Winnie waylaid him at the foot of the stairs, eager for a romp, which romp resulted in Winnie, while being tossed high in air, throwing back her head and striking him a tremendous blow in the eye with it, so that he set her hastily down with an exclamation of pain, and put his hand to his face.

"You've done it now, Winnie; blinded me," he said.

"Oh, Henry, I am so sorry!" sobbed Winnie. "And they won't let me go to Long's tea-party to-morrow; it was only on Sunday I made Ingram Swaynestone's nose bleed."

"Never mind, darling," said Everard, kissing and soothing her; "it was not your fault at all."

Then he promised to let no one know of his black eye, and to do his best to cure it; to which intent he procured raw meat from the kitchen, and went to his room, taking Winnie with him to help him unpack the parcel, which contained some choice white flowers. These he bid the child take to her sister at once, while he shut himself

up, and tried to subdue the rising inflamma-
tion in the bruised eye to the best of his
ability.

He was anxious to avoid such an ornament
as a black eye on his own account, as well
as the child's, since a black eye does not
improve a man's appearance at a ball, nor
is it in keeping with popular ideas of a newly
accepted lover. So he doctored himself till
it was time to get ready for dinner, and then,
seeing the grey suit lie on the chair as he
had placed it in the morning, he sponged the
green stain away from it. Scarcely had he
done this when he saw other stains, some still
wet, and, procuring some fresh water, sponged
these also. The water was red when he
finished.

"Blood," he thought, being well used to
such stains. "Did I cut myself anywhere, I
wonder?"

He did not, however, waste much thought
on this trivial incident, but sponged the
garments clean in his tidy way, and left the
crimsoned water in the basin, where it subse-

quently gave Martha, the housemaid, what
she described as a turn. Then he made his
appearance in the drawing-room, carefully
avoiding the lights, and gave rather a lame
account of himself since his return from the
fruitless errand to Widow Dove's. He was
rewarded for his labour on Lilian's behalf, by
the sweetest smile in the world, and was
enchanted to observe at dinner that Lilian
wore one of the white roses from his bouquet
in her dress.

Cyril did not appear at dinner; he sent
word that one of his bad headaches had come
on, and begged that he might be undisturbed
for the night.

"Poor dear Cyril!" said Lilian; "it is so
hard for a man to have headaches. His are
like mine; nothing but quiet heals them."

"Their very headaches are twins," Mr.
Maitland observed. "Why, Henry," he
added, "what have you done to your eye?
You appear to have been in the wars, man."

Winnie, who was standing by the fire,
here threw an imploring glance at Henry,

and completely scattered what few talents he had ever possessed for dissimulation.

"I—I—I knocked my head against something in the dark," he stammered; "I—it was purely accidental."

"What a nasty blow!" said Lilian, observing it; "you will have a black eye. What a pity! Ah, sir! perhaps that accounts for your rudeness to me this evening."

"My rudeness, Lilian? What can you mean?" asked Henry.

"Yes, your incivility to me, and also to Mark Antony, who was actually doing you the honour of running to meet you—the haughty Mark himself. Think of that!"

"I can only apologize to both with the deepest humility," he replied, stroking the petted animal, who was dining with his usual urbane condescension at Lilian's side; "but indeed I am quite innocent, having seen neither you nor puss since you started for Swaynestone."

Then Lilian told how at tea-time, on passing from the back regions towards the drawing-room, accompanied by her usual body-guard, Mark Antony, she had seen Henry run across the back hall towards the staircase; had called to him about Widow Dove's commission; while the cat, with a mew of delight, had bounded after him. He had rushed on, however, in the dusk, a grey, ghost-like figure, and flitted up the stairs to his room, followed by Mark, whom he expelled ignominiously, shutting the door after him.

" You must be under some delusion," replied Henry, utterly confounded. " I saw no cat when I came in."

" It was growing very dark," Lilian said, " and Martha was late in lighting the hall-lamp to-night, for which, indeed, I afterwards rebuked her."

" The lamps were lighted——" Henry began, and then stopped at the sight of Winnie, who was gesticulating in an agonized manner behind her mother's chair. " This sounds extremely ghost-like," he added; " I hope it bodes me no misfortune. It must have been my wraith, Lilian."

"It sounds rather eerie, certainly," interposed Mr. Maitland. "Lilian dear, I hope you are not going to take to seeing people's wraiths. It gives me the most fearful jumps to think of."

"I am creeping from head to foot," added Mrs. Maitland, laughing; "and on the last night of the year, too. Dr. Everard, what prescriptions have you for young ladies who take to ghost-seeing?"

"I am going to ask you for another cutlet, sir. My appetite will convince you that I, at least, am no illusion, but a substantial reality," said Henry, instead of replying.

"There never was any deception about you, Harry lad," returned Mr. Maitland, cordially; "you were always real."

The evening which ensued ought to have been very happy, but somehow it was not. A vague uneasiness was in the air; Cyril's absence created a void in the family party, and the children, who were permitted to stay up for the New Year, grew tired, and consequently tiresome. Mr. Maitland, when he recovered from his after-dinner nap, which was unusually long, read them one of Dickens's Christmas tales, and although it was pleasant to Henry to sit by Lilian and watch her beautiful white hands at their busy task of embroidering some silken flowers, he was not sorry when, the servants having been assembled in the drawing-room, a pleasant clinking of glasses was heard, and, the usual ceremonies of toasting and hand-shaking gone through, the bells began drowsily chiming the Old Year out from the belfry hard by.

They all went into the hall then, Mr. Maitland opened the door wide to let the New Year in, and Lilian and Henry, hand-in-hand, gazed trustfully out into the starry sky to meet it, their hearts full of the sweetest hopes.

When Henry went to his room soon after, he could not refrain from opening Cyril's door, which adjoined his own, and just looking in, thinking he might be asleep. He pushed the door very softly, and introduced his head. Only a faint light was burning from one candle, and by this dim ray he saw Cyril kneeling half-dressed before a picture of the Crucifixion. His face was hidden in his hands, and he was sobbing in a low, suppressed way.

Henry shut the door softly, and stealthily withdrew, vexed at his own intrusion. "That is not the way to cure the headache," he mused, half awed at the manner in which the young priest received the New Year. Yet who could venture to say that watching and fasting and tearful contrition were not eminently fitting, in one set apart for holy functions, at such a season? "I wonder," Everard continued to speculate, "what infinitesimal peccadilloes the poor lad is mourning with all that expenditure of nervous energy?" Then he thought of his own weaknesses and shortcomings, and felt pitchy black in contrast with a soul so white.

CHAPTER XI.

THE wheelwright's house stood just on the
crest of the steep little hill which carries the
pilgrim down into the village of Malbourne
with a rapid acceleration of pace, and which
ends where the four roads meet. The Sun
Inn stands at one corner, facing the incoming
pilgrim cheerfully on its left; and opposite
this tidy hostelry stands a sign-post apparently waving four gaunt arms distractedly,
and seeming to bid the wayfarer pause
beneath the thatched roof of the little inn,
whether his journey's end lie onwards over
the high-road, or oblige him to turn aside
through the village by church and Rectory.

On the traveller's right, facing him, is a
cottage, and facing that is the wheelwright's
yard, full of timber and waggons half built or

broken. The wheelwright's dwelling, standing above the grassy yard, commands a fine view of the village nestled under the down and the sweeping parklands of Northover on one side, and on the other looks over an undulating landscape to the sea. It is a cheery little house, pleasantly shaded by a couple of shapely lindens in front, and close to the high-road, upon which its front windows and deep-timbered porch give.

On New Year's Eve the wheelwright's windows were all lighted up, and there was even a lantern at the little front wicket, which gazed out like a friendly eye, as if to bid people enter and make merry within, and threw a yellow fan-shaped radiance on the steep road without. The porch door was open, and disclosed a passage lighted by a candle in a tin sconce adorned with holly. On one side, an open door revealed the chill dignities of the best parlour, which not even a blazing fire and abundance of holly-berries could quite warm.

On a haircloth sofa in this state apartment

sat Mrs. Hale, of Malbourne Mill, and Mrs.
Wax, the schoolmaster's wife, both exceed-
ingly upright, and both holding a handkerchief of Gargantuan dimensions over the
hands they crossed in their laps. Opposite,
in a horsehair arm-chair, sat an elderly lady
in a plum-coloured silk gown, gold chain,
and a splendid cap, also very upright, and
also holding a Gargantuan handkerchief.
This was Mrs. Cave, the wife of a small
farmer in the neighbourhood.

Each lady's face wore a resigned expression,
mingled with the calm exultation natural to
people who know themselves to be the most
aristocratic persons in a social gathering.
Each realized that *Würde hat Bürde*, and felt
herself equal to the occasion; each paused,
before making or replying to an observation,
to consider the most genteel subjects of
conversation and the most genteel language
in which to clothe them.

" Remorkably fine weather for the time of
year, ladies," observed Mrs. Hale, soothing
her soul by the pleasant rustle her shot-silk

gown made when she smoothed it, and
regretting that her gold chain was not so
new-fashioned as Mrs. Cave's; while, on the
other hand, she experienced a delicious
comfort in meditating on the superiority of
her brooch, which was a large flat pebble in
a gold frame.

"Indeed, mem, it is most seasonable,
though trying for delicate chestes," returned
Mrs. Cave, with her finest company smile,
after which a pause of three minutes ensued.

"Some say the frost is on the breek," continued Mrs. Hale, wondering if it would be
genteel to ask Mrs. Cave how much her cap
cost. She had an agonized suspicion that it
would not.

After five minutes, Mrs. Wax, whose com-
parative youth and lower rank occasioned
her some diffidence, took up her parable in
the following genteel manner :—" Her ladyship was observing this marning—— "

But what her ladyship was observing was
never revealed to man, since at that moment,
Widow Hale, the host's mother, came burst-

ing in, stout, healthy, and red-faced, her cap
slightly awry, and called out in her hearty,
wholesome voice—

" Well, now, my dears, and how are *you*
getting on? I'm that harled up with so
many about, I ain't had a minute to ast after
ye all. Mary Ann, my dear, give me a kiss
do, and a hearty welcome to you all, and a
kiss all round, and do make yourselves at
home. Now, is the tea to your liking?
This best teapot ain't much at drawing. I
ain't much of a one for best things myself;
well enough for looking at, and just to say
you've got them, but give me work-a-day
things for comfort. There ain't above half
the company come yet, and Mary Ann upset
about the pies for supper. Do just as you
would at home, and you will please me. If
there ain't dear old Granfer coming in, bless
his heart! Come in, Granfer, and kindly
welcome."

And so saying, the kind soul bustled out,
and relieved Granfer of his hat, while her
daughter-in-law, the actual hostess, came to

do the honours of the best parlour, bringing in three more female guests of distinction, who were much awed by the appalling gentility of the three already assembled, and a little inclined to regret their own social importance.

Granfer and the widow, in the mean time, entered the great kitchen, a long, low, white-washed room, with heavy beams across the ceiling, a stone floor, and a wide hearth with a wood fire burning between dogs upon it. The ceiling and walls wore their everyday decoration of hams, guns, a spit, various cooking utensils, a tiny bookshelf, and a large dresser, well garnished with crockery and pewters, together with their festal Christmas adorning of holly, fir, and mistle-toe, and a round dozen of tin sconces bearing tallow candles. There was an oaken settle on one side the chimney corner, into the cosiest nook of which Granfer deposited his bent form with a sigh of content, and gazed round upon the assembled guests with benevolence.

On a long table on trestles at one end of the room was spread a solid meal, consisting of a huge ham, own brother to those depending in rich brown abundance from the ceiling; a south-country, skim-milk cheese, finely marbled with greenish blue veins, and resembling Stilton in reduced circumstances; a great yellow and brown mass of roast beef; a huge pie; several big brown blocks of plumcake; and some vast loaves of white home-baked bread and pats of fresh butter. The forks were of steel, and black-handled like the knives; and the spoons, of which there was a dearth, were pewter. A deficiency of tea-cups suggested to Corporal Tom Hale the agreeable expedient of sharing one between a lady and a gentleman, which was hailed with applause by his naval brother, and immediately acted upon.

For those guests who looked upon tea as an enervating beverage, there was ample provision in the shape of various brown and yellow jugs filled with ale from the cask Tom and Jim had procured for the occasion; and it was generally understood that liquor of a still more comforting nature was held in reserve to stimulate conviviality at a later hour. The blacksmith, Straun, the clerk, Stevens, with their wives and families, were there; also Baines, the discontented tailor, and the husbands of the best-parlour ladies.

The wheelwright's wife, a comely woman of thirty, and his sister, a blooming damsel some ten years younger, ran to and fro with flushed faces among the guests, while the widow made herself ubiquitous.

The uniforms of Tom and Jim, with those of three or four artillerymen from the neighbouring forts, and the red coats of a couple of linesmen, together with the bright ribbons of the women, lent colour and variety to the monotony of black coats and smock-frocks, and upon the whole the wheelwright's kitchen presented as cheery and animated a sight as one would wish to see on a New Year's Eve. Nor was a town element wanting in the rustic gathering; for just as tea was in full swing, and little Dickie Stevens—

whose tea lay in the future, after the serving of his elders—was supplying the place of a band by playing hymn-tunes on his concertina, a taxed-cart drove up, and deposited two chilled mortals from Oldport, Mr. and Mrs. Wells, greengrocers, and related, by some inextricable family complications known only in that remote south-country district, more or less to nearly all the company.

Tea being finished, pipes were produced, also ale, and there was wild work in a dimly lighted quarter of the kitchen, where the Hale brothers had cunningly arranged unexpected mistletoe, and whence smothered shrieks of laughter and sounds as of ears being vigorously boxed issued every now and then.

The odd part about the mistletoe business was the extreme gullibility of the ladies, who were by far too guileless to profit by the experience of others in that dangerous region, and suffered themselves to be decoyed thither on the flimsiest pretexts, and betrayed the utmost surprise and indignation at the

kissing which invariably ensued. As for
Tom and Jim, they went to work with a
business-like determination to kiss every girl
in the room, and several respectable matrons
into the bargain. It was about this time
that the artillery sergeant and the wheelwright's pretty sister Patty vanished, and
were subsequently discovered at the front
door, enjoying the soft December breeze and
studying astronomy, a study which produced
the happiest subsequent results, and set the
Malbourne bells chiming in the spring of the
coming year.

So large and successful a party had not
been held in Malbourne for many a year, the
predominance of the military element greatly
contributing to its success; for the sons of
Mars excelled not only in the art of pleasing
the fairer sex, which has in all ages been
considered their special function, but possessed
many other accomplishments of social value.
A very pretty bit of fencing was exhibited
between a red and a blue coat, and Corporal
Tom snuffed candles with a pistol, amid

shrieks of terrified delight from the women.
One soldier sang a comic, another a sentimental, song; and when little Dick Stevens
was perched on a table, and warbled out,
" Rosalie, the Prairie Flower," and "Wait for
the Waggon," to the accompaniment of Wax's
clarionet and Baines's violin, the kitchen
ceiling trembled and threatened to drop its
quivering hams and hollies at the powerful
chorus furnished by these stalwart warriors,
and the gentility of the best parlour was
finally melted by it to such a deliquescence
as to mingle freely with the vulgar currents
circulating in the kitchen.

Indeed, village talent was quite in the shade
during the first part of the evening, and the
discreet Corporal Tom observed such deprecia-
tion on the faces of the village genuises that
he resolved to put off asking for the recitation
with which he knew a certain warrior to be
primed until a later hour, and created a
diversion by proposing a game of Turn the
Trencher, which absorbed the children and
younger people at one end of the room, and

left the circle of elders round the chimney free to converse or visit the best parlour, where fruit and sherry wine were laid out, as they pleased.

" I seen young Mr. Maitland in Oldport to-day," observed the town greengrocer's lady, one of the fireside circle, by way of furnishing the town news to her rustic friends.

"Now, did you, Mrs. Wells ? " returned her host. " Ah ! so you zeen he ? "

"Yes, Mr. Hale ; I seen him go into the bank opposite, and stay there—oh !· I should think a good hour," continued Mrs. Wells, adjusting her cap-ribbons with a complacent sense of their splendour. " He's grown more personable than ever ; but he do look ill, poor young gentleman, to be sure—that white and thin ! "

" That's living in Lunnun," said Hale ; " Lunnun takes it out of a man. I never held with going to Lunnun myself. Never knowed any good come of it."

" Ah, you don't know everythink, Jacob

Hale!" said Granfer, benevolently. " 'Tain't, zo to zay, nateral to a man as gives hisself entirely to wheels. You doos your best, but more zense can't come out of ye than the Almighty have a put in. Na-a. You don't know everythink, Jacob Hale, I zays."

The profundity of this remark produced a deep impression, particularly upon the wheel-wright, who appeared to think he had received a great compliment from Granfer, and rekindled his pipe at the burning gorse on the hearth with a beatified air.

" Zeems as though zummat had been a-taking of it out of Mr. Cyril," observed the blacksmith, thoughtfully.

" 'Tain't, zo to zay, Lunnon, Jarge Straun," replied Granfer, solemnly. " No, Jarge Straun; 'tain't Lunnon, as you med zay. I zes to Bill Stevens 's marning, I zays, ' Bill,' I zays, zays I, ' brains is the matter wi' Mr. Cyril,' I zays, ' that's what's the matter wi' he ; ' " and Granfer's keen grey eyes took a survey of all the listening, stolid faces, and he experienced a keen sense of enjoyment, as he leant forwards, his hands crossed on his staff, and felt that he was getting into regular conversational swing. "Ay, that's what I zed, zure enough," he added.

"Brains!" repeated Straun, thoughtfully. "I never yeared of nobody dying of brains, as I knows on."

"You ain't a yeered everythink, Jarge Straun," returned Granfer, severely. "Ay, you med mark my words, it all hruns to brains wi' Mr. Cyril; there ain't, as you med zay, nothing left to hrun to vlesh and vat, whatever he med put inzide of hisself. Mankind is like the vlower o' the vield: where it all hruns to vlower, there ain't, zo to zay, zo much leaf as you med swear by; then, agen, I tell 'ee, where it all runs to leaf, you can't expect no vlower to speak on. Look at broccoli!"

Here Granfer, being fairly launched, struck out from personal to general observations, and thence, at the prompting of his grandson, to the hoary regions of history.

"Ay, I minds Boney, to be zure—well I

minds he ; " and he related the oft-told tale of the frequent scares the inhabitants of those coasts received, sometimes by authentic rumours of Bonaparte's appearance at sea, sometimes by the accidental or mistaken kindling of the beacons on every prominent headland and on the downs, where a watch was kept day and night for the appearance of the dreaded foe.

He told how the wealthy farmers sent their silver and other valuables, sometimes including even their women and children under the latter head, inland for safety— most of them, apparently, having first consulted Granfer on the subject—in consequence of Bonaparte's rumoured descents on that fated coast; also of the rousing of the volunteers at the dead of night on one of these occasions—of their march to the seashore, and their all getting lost on the way, and arriving next morning on a scene of profound peace. Then came the great smuggler story, and the tragic history of the loss of the ship *Halifax*, the crew and

passengers of which lay buried in the wind-
swept churchyard near the fatal shore which
wrecked them. Five young women were
among those washed ashore and subsequently
buried, and their appearance, as Granfer saw
them, lying pale and beautiful side by side
awaiting burial, was the climax of this story;
after delivering it he usually paused and
looked round for some moments with working
lips to enjoy the silence of the interested
listeners.

Having thus got his audience, which consisted mainly of village seniors, well in hand,
Granfer began, to the accompaniment of the
young people's continuous laughter, somewhat
softened by distance, to play upon their love
of the marvellous and the horrible, and produced some delightful creeps by his eerie
tales; and finally landed himself in his re-
nowned narrative of his midnight adventure
upon Down End, a bleak, storm-stricken
eminence, where the last man gibbeted in
these parts, a truculent villain, with a most
romantic history, then swung in chains.

Granfer had been belated on a moonless, cloudy night, had wandered far in the cutting wind, and had begun to guess that he had at last done with the downs, and reached the well-known Down End—an unpleasant spot for a midnight stroll, since, besides the unwelcome presence of the murderer on his gibbet, an extensive chalk quarry there supplied an array of little precipices high enough to cost any one slipping over the edge his life.

Granfer had arrived at a vague mass looming through the darkness, a dim *something*, which he conjectured to be the sign-post, an erection which shared the same eminence with the gibbet at many yards distance from it, and was about to strike a light with the flint and steel in his pocket to a weird accompaniment of shrieks and moans and unholy riot of clankings and hissings, which might be only the voices of the midnight storm, but, on the other hand, *might be* what Granfer wisely left to his hearers' imaginations, when "all on a zuddent there comes a girt bang on the shoulders of me, vlint and

steel vlies out of my hands, and down I goos,
vlat as a vlounder on my väace, wi' zummat
atop o' me," the old man was saying, his
wrinkled face and keen eyes lighted by the
blazing gorse fire and his own imagination,
while Straun and Hale, and the other worthies,
with open mouths, staring eyes, and dropped
pipes, and the women, with various contor-
tions of visage and extensive clasping of
shivering hands, gazed with tense, strained
attention upon the withered, eager countenance, when the door burst open, and William
Grove, supported by Corporal Tom, staggered
into the kitchen, white-faced and trembling,
and fell into a chair placed for him in the
centre of the room, clapping his hands con-
vulsively upon his knees, and exclaiming at
intervals, " O Lard ! O Lard 'a massey ! "
and the sudden apparition, coming thus upon
strained nerves and excited imaginations,
produced a most alarming effect.

The women screamed and clung to one
another ; the men uttered ejaculations ; the
game of Turn the Trencher broke up in dis-

may, and the players came clustering round the
distracted Grove; while the services of the
military were called into requisition to soothe
the terrors and agitations of the prettiest girls,
the gallant sergeant finding it necessary to
place his arm round the blooming form of
Miss Patty Hale for the distressed damsel's
support.

"Lard 'a massey! Willum Grove," exclaimed Granfer at last, with impatience, " if
you ain't got nothink better to zay than Lard
'a massey, you med zo well bide quiet, I tell
'ee. Lard love 'ee, Willum, you never had
no zense to speak on, but you be clane *dunch*
now. Ay, Willum be clane *dunch*," he added;
while the astute Tom, who said that William
had come flying in at the porch door (where
the gallant corporal had been helping pretty
Miss Cave to admire the moon), and could be
prevailed upon to make no other observation
than that so scornfully censured by Granfer,
assisted the waggoner's faculties by a timely
draught of ale. After disposing of this, and
drying his mouth with the back of his hand,

William recovered slightly and found his
tongue.

"Lard 'a massey on us all!" he cried;
"they bin an' done for poor Ben Lee."

"Done for him!" cried a chorus of voices
in various tones of horror and dismay.

"Done var en, zure enough!" repeated
William, rocking himself backward and forward, in a strange contrast to his usual
stolidity. "We bin an' vound the body!"

It was even so. Ben Lee left his home at
dinner-time, and had not returned. At tea-
time, Mrs. Lee was returning in the dusk
from an errand to Malbourne, and met a
hurrying figure clad in grey, as she came
through the fields beneath the wood, which
was on the crest of the hill above the Temple.
She found only Alma in the house, and after
waiting with more discontent than disquiet,
she concluded that work had delayed her
husband, and finally took her tea and seated
herself at her needlework by the fire.

At half-past seven Sir Lionel and Lady
Swaynestone, with their daughter, were

dressed for a dinner-party and awaiting the
arrival of the carriage, which had been
ordered at that hour. But no carriage
appeared, and a message to the stables
elicited the news that the coachman had not
been there since the afternoon, when Ingram
Swaynestone chanced to have seen him near
his home. A messenger to the Temple returned with the tidings that he had not
been home; and then Judkins asked for an
audience with Sir Lionel, which resulted in
a search-party being sent forth to find the
missing man, whose habits were regular and
punctual.

William Grove, who chanced to be on some
errand to Swaynestone for his master before
going to the wheelwright's party, assisted
in the search, and was with Judkins when
Lee was discovered quite dead in the wood
above his home. There were no signs of
any struggle on the hard frozen path, from
whence his body had evidently been dragged
into the fern and brush, whither it was traced
by the marks on the rime-covered moss and

the disorder of the ferns and brambles. A slight wound on the face, which had bled, but could not have killed him, was the only sign of violence at first seen.

The lights were not extinguished at Swayne-stone House till nearly dawn. Sir Lionel, who was a magistrate, set to work at once to investigate the fatal affair, the police were immediately informed, and every member of the Swaynestone household was closely questioned, as well as Mrs. Lee. Poor Alma could not be subjected to much inter-rogation, and was not in a position to throw any light upon the tragedy. Death was not the only visitor at the Temple; a new life, scarcely less tragic than the death, began there on that fatal night, and the New Year rose upon sorrow and dismay in hall and cottage.

It took long to extract what he knew of the affair from William Grove, but this was at length accomplished, amid varied comment and ejaculation. Granfer said no further word until the whole truth had been elicited,

and then upon the first favourable pause he
looked round with an air of great solemnity,
and took up his parable thus : " You med
all mark my words.   Zomebody'll hae to
swing for this yere.   Ay, I've said it, and
I'll zay it agen : zomebody'll hae to swing."

CHAPTER XII.

NEXT to the divine sweetness of youthful love, nothing so completely charms and enthrals us as the rapid development of new ideas and the swift inrush of fresh knowledge in the spring-time of life. How the world widens to the eager student, what vast and endless horizons open out to his gaze, as he acquires fresh knowledge! What a sense of power his thoughts give him as they draw together from the vagueness of scattered speculations, and take definite shape before him! Love unlocks the gate of a yet undiscovered world of emotion, which has its higher and lower circles, its purgatory and paradise, and its endless possibilities beyond; knowledge and ripening thought rend the obscuring veils from the illimitable universe.

The enthusiastic delight of fresh discovery is in both cases the very elixir of life; nay, it is life itself.

On the last day of the year, Everard discovered the new world of love; and on New Year's morning, under the stimulus of a fresh happiness, a theory, after which he had long been groping with many a vague surmise and hazardous hypothesis, interrupted by hopeless gaps in evidence, suddenly revealed itself complete and flawless before him. It came like an electric shock, with such a happy flash of inspiration that he was obliged to pause in his dressing to take in the results of the unconscious cerebration which his studies and speculations had set up, while tears of joy rushed to his eyes. Clear and distinct as it was to his own mind, he knew that years of patient labour and minute scientific investigation must pass before he could present it to other minds, but he knew also that, once verified, it would make an epoch in the study of physiology.

Such a superabundance of happiness as

Everard's might well excite the malignity of envious gods, and would have prompted an ancient Greek to throw away some precious thing in all haste. But being a Christian Englishman, Everard did not follow the example of Polycrates; nay, had he been a Greek of old days, he would never have imputed envy or malignity to the strong immortals. Strength was to him a guarantee of goodness, because his own strength made him noble and kind; it made him also pitiful to the malice and spite of weak things.

Full of this new rapture, his eyes hazy with abstraction, as the eyes of dreamers are hazy with dreams, Everard went forth to meet the New Year's new joy like one borne upon clouds, and reached the breakfast-room just at the end of prayers. Mr. Maitland according to custom, was dismissing the maids with a kind good morning and New Year's wish, when Eliza, whose face was stained with tears, paused with a spasmodic, " Oh, please, sir ! "

" You are discomposed, Eliza," said Mr.

Maitland, gently, while he looked round and observed similar perturbation on the faces of the other maids. " Nothing wrong, I hope ? "

" Poor Ben Lee ! " sobbed Eliza, resorting to her handkerchief.

" He was found dead, sir," added Martha, the housemaid, her grief, which was sincere, tempered by a certain delight in the tragically impressive.

" It was Stevens brought the news," added the cook, who was also not impervious to the pleasure of communicating disastrous intelligence.

" Found dead ! My good girls ! In Heaven's name, where ? when ? Oh, surely not ! Where *is* Stevens ? " cried Mr. Maitland, as much agitated as the heart of woman could desire. " Oh, those poor Lees ! What trouble ! what trouble ! "

" It was last night, sir," continued Eliza, much refreshed by her master's perturbation, and by the copious tears with which she had accompanied the broken narrative. " Sir Lionel had lanterns sent out for him."

"He did not die in his bed, then?" the deep voice of Everard broke in.

"He was hid away in the wood," replied Martha; "and they do say——"

"I must go to the Temple at once," interrupted Mr. Maitland, starting off to get his hat, with an injunction to the women not to talk over the tragedy, which he might as well have addressed to the wind.

Lilian with great difficulty succeeded in keeping him back until she had made him drink some coffee and take a little food, when he started off at railroad speed, bidding her tell the clerk there would be no service that morning. Then Henry and Lilian and the two children sat down to a melancholy breakfast, and the discussion of the tragedy, of which they gathered from the servants as much as William Grove had communicated on the previous night, together with a fine growth of conjecture and exaggeration.

"Poor Alma!" sighed Lilian, when her father was gone. "Oh, Henry! what do you think of it?"

" I am afraid it looks rather dark," returned Henry, not observing the entrance of Eliza with a hot dish. " Lee's behaviour, when last I saw him, was most unaccountable. His trouble evidently preyed on his mind, poor fellow."

" Oh, Henry ! what do you mean ? Not—— "

" An unhinged mind quickly turns to suicide," replied Henry, suddenly checking himself as he became aware of the wide gaze of Winnie's eyes immediately opposite him.

Five minutes after, the whole of Malbourne knew that Dr. Everard had received the intelligence with little surprise, and at once ascribed it to suicide.

Cyril had started for Woodlands before breakfast, leaving a charming note of New Year's wishes for everybody, and saying that it was incumbent on him to go to Woodlands at once, to apologize for his incivility in not meeting Marion on the previous day.

" What a devoted lover ! " Mr. Maitland had observed, on hearing the note read.

" Well, man has but one spring-time, though the birds renew their youth every year."

" I think, papa," said Winnie, in one of those sudden visitations of acuteness which befall little girls occasionally, " that Cyril is not so devoted to loving as to being loved."

And Lilian knew that the child had hit on her brother's weak point.

After breakfast, Everard accompanied Lilian and the children on a visit to the invalid donkey and other dumb dependents. It was pleasant to see Lilian in the poultry-yard. When she entered the yard she gave a little coo, and a flock of pigeons, preening themselves aloft on gable and roof in the sunshine, came fluttering down, a rustling cloud of white wings, and settled upon her till she seemed a parody on Lot's wife, a pillar of birds instead of salt, while the more adventurous fowls sprang up and pecked the grain from her basket and her hands, till she scattered pigeons, fowls, and all, with a light " Hish ! " and wave of her arms.

Everard, the children, and the two dogs

stood apart to watch this little scene, Everard smoking tranquilly, and delighting in the picture of Lilian involved in her cloud of dove-like wings. During this progress he told her eagerly of the theory which had been born in his brain that morning, and they both discussed it, Lilian being sufficiently grounded in science to comprehend something of the importance of the subject, and having, moreover, the receptive intellect which readily admits half-grasped notions.

"We shall have to work hard for this," Everard said, knowing that Lilian would willingly take her share of the toil.

"It will be well worth hard work," she replied joyously; "but I have other work now, so I must go in. No; I have not told mother," she added, in reply to a whispered question from Henry; "I would rather it came from you."

"And I have had no opportunity as yet." he said. "So I have to skate with these scamps, have I? Very well; but join us as soon as you can, Lilian."

"And mind you bring some cake," added
Lennie, who was nothing if not practical;
and the children, hanging one on each of
Everard's hands, danced joyously off into
Northover Park, where they were to skate
on a piece of water a quarter of a mile off.

Just as they entered the gate by the lodge,
Lyster Garrett was leaving it. He looked at
Henry with some surprise, and received his
greeting very stiffly.

"Oh, do come and skate, Lyster!" cried
Lennie; "then you can help me, and Winnie
can have Henry to herself."

"I am going to Swaynestone," Garrett
said. "This is a sad business of Lee's. Foul
play, I fear;" and he looked searchingly at
Everard.

"Foul play?" returned Everard. "Nonsense! Why, I suppose poor Lee never had
an enemy in his life."

"He had one," said Garrett, with marked
emphasis. "I should strongly recommend
that person to make himself scarce."

" Lee was not a man to make enemies, poor

fellow," replied Everard. " It will all come out at the inquest, no doubt. Mr. Maitland is gone to the Temple to comfort the poor widow."

And they passed on, Everard wondering what on earth was the matter with young Garrett, who was studying for the Bar, and was rather inclined to look upon human existence as raw material to be worked up in courts of justice.

" The world doesn't *look* much older than it did yesterday, Henry," observed Winnie, thoughtfully ; " yet it's sixty-three, and yesterday it was only sixty-two."

Henry did not reply, but looked reflectively at the frozen landscape and clouded sky, whence the sun had been shining half an hour before. There was a vague misgiving within him ; Garrett's hints flung a shroud of dark conjecture over the Lee tragedy, which he had forgotten for the moment. The world did look older to him, and it seemed a whole year since yesterday. But the pond was soon reached, and the children's skates and his own had to be fitted on at the expense of freezing fingers and stagnant blood, which a few turns in the biting air set right again. Then the Garrett ladies appeared, and there was quite a little party on the ice, and the children having by this time learnt to go alone, Henry indulged himself in some artistic skating, and the world grew young again, and he did not observe that Miss Garrett and her sister declined all his offers of assistance, and avoided him as much as the small extent of the little lake would permit.

"I am not sure that I shall marry Ingram Swaynestone, after all," Winnie observed to Lilian, when she arrived with the promised cake in an hour's time. "I think pw'aps I shall have Henwy when I gwow up."

"There was nobody in the world like Ingram yesterday," Lilian laughed; "so I suppose your skating instructions have been more successful than his, Henry."

"This is rather a dismal New Years morning," Lilian said to Henry, who was busily engaged in fitting on her skates.

"Those poor Lees haunt me, and the servants say there are such dreadful surmises about Ben's death. I wish Cyril were here. I wonder what he is doing?"

Cyril at that moment was in the library at Woodlands, comfortably seated in a deep armchair by a blazing fire. The laity of the male kind were shooting; Marion, and her sister, Mrs. Whiteford, were busily employed with the other ladies in decorations and arrangements for the impending ball. Cyril had taken refuge in the library with a book that he was utterly unable to read, and was sorry to find that George Everard had followed his example.

The Rev. George had assumed that attitude on the hearthrug which means conversation, and the disposition of his coat-tails was such as forebodes a long discourse, as Cyril observed with inward groans. Cyril's face was strained and haggard; his mind was in the tense, over-wrought condition which craves solitude and repose; and he racked his brains for some pretext to escape from his brother-clergyman, who had the advantage of being his senior by many years, and whose theology was of a kind to fill Cyril with despair, since George belonged to the straitest sect of the Evangelicals.

Mr. Everard began by commenting upon his young brother's worn appearance, and accusing him of fasting.

" I fasted," replied Cyril, " because I was too unwell to eat. And if I received the New Year with watching and prayer, you will surely allow that I might have done worse."

" Truly. I could wish many to follow your example, Maitland ; but not to the injury of this fleshly tabernacle, as I fear you have done. Such misdirected zeal amounts to excess, and that will-worship against which we are cautioned. You played a very poor part at breakfast, I observed."

Cyril smiled, for he had observed, on his part, George Everard's vigorous onslaught upon his father's well-spread breakfast-table, and he replied that his lack of appetite was due to his own folly in taking a long walk

fasting after a day of headache. "Indeed,
I am thoroughly knocked up," he added
wearily.

"My dear young friend," continued George,
solemnly, "I have become deeply interested
in you. I perceive that you are a very
precious vessel."

In spite of his weariness, and the strange
hunted look that made him appear to start
at every sound, as if expecting evil tidings,
Cyril's face kindled and gained an added
charm at these words. Appreciation was
the very breath of life to him, and he felt
that he had hitherto thought too slightingly
of George, who perhaps, after all, could not
help being evangelical, and consequently
rather slangy in his religious conversation.
He made a graceful allusion to their impending relationship, thanked George for his good
opinion, and expressed a hope that they
might know more of each other before long.

"I have wrestled in prayer for you," continued the elder priest. "I shall continue to
wrestle, that you may come to know the

truth, and that you may have strength to resist the seductions of the Scarlet Woman. I observe great powers in you—singular powers ; powers that may effect much in the vineyard, if you only devote them to your Master's service ; powers which, unsanctified, will lead you into great temptations."

" I am in for it," thought Cyril, who disliked listening to other people's sermons as much as doctors object to taking their own prescriptions ; " he is wound up for at least six heads." But his face wore the most winning expression of interest and the deference due to one so much older in the ministry than himself, while he replied modestly that he was aware that some talents had been vouchsafed him, and did not intend to hide them in a napkin, but that he thought perhaps his dear brother rated him too highly in the kindness of his heart.

At which Everard smiled paternally, and proceeded to speak of Cyril's gifts—his agreeable manner and power of winning hearts, his eloquence, his intellectual polish, and his

musical and flexible voice, and pointed out
to him the peculiar power these would give
him in his ministerial capacity.

"Not that these mere carnal gifts are
anything in themselves," he continued; "they
are but nets to catch men. The nets are not
necessary, but it pleases the Lord to work by
means, and those to whom much is given will
have much to answer for. In short, you have
very singular opportunities of doing good
work in the vineyard. I am thankful that
you have been moved to enter the ministry.
You might have had a more brilliant career
in a worldly calling. But what you have
undertaken is worth any sacrifice. And no
man, having once put his hand to the plough,
may dare to look back."

George Everard was not destitute of the
human weakness that leads us to believe in
the value of our own good advice, but he
would have been rather startled if he could
have known the powerful effect his words
had upon his susceptible and impulsive
listener's mind.

" I *have* put my hand to the plough," said Cyril, taking away the hands in which he had buried his haggard face during this exordium, and speaking in those deep, strong chest-notes which so stirred the fibre of his listeners' hearts; "I will never turn back. I call you to witness, George Everard, in the face of high Heaven, that I will never turn back, and that I will make any and every sacrifice for the sake of this my high calling and vocation."

Cyril rose from his seat as he spoke, and raised one hand with an impressive gesture. All the languor and dejection vanished from his face and form; a dazzle of pale blue fire came from his eyes; his every feature kindled; his whole being expressed an intensity of feeling that almost frightened Everard, who felt something like a child playing with matches and suddenly kindling a wood-pile. He could only ejaculate faintly, "My dear young friend!" while Cyril paced the room with firm strides and loftily erect head, a thing of grace and spirit-like beauty, and at last paused in front of George with such a glance of fire as seemed to pierce through and through the soul of the elder man, and offered him his hand, saying, " Do you bear me witness ? "

" I do indeed," faltered the other, overcome by the sight of an emotion beyond his conception, accustomed though he was to a purely sentimental form of religion ; and he pressed Cyril's fevered hand in his own cool one, uttering some words of prayer and blessing, thinking that possibly one of the sudden conversions he so constantly preached about, and so rarely discovered any traces of in actual life, had taken place.

" Your words," said Cyril, quietly, after a time, " were like a spark to a train of gunpowder. They came at a moment of internal wrestling, and helped me to a decision."

George Everard replied that he was blest in being the unworthy instrument of speaking a word in season, and proceeded to admonish his convert at length ; while Cyril, with all the fire quenched in his look and

bearing, sat drooping and haggard beneath
the cold, unimpassioned gaze of his counsellor,
busied with his own thoughts, and occasionally smiling a little inward smile as the
well-worn phrases and various allusions to
the Scarlet Woman fell on his wearied ear.

"In conclusion, dear Cyril," George said
at length, "I must bid you beware of
women."

Cyril started and flushed, but Everard
smiled and continued—

"Do not mistake me. You have hitherto
had no temptation from that source; the
monastic discipline of your life at St. Chad's,
however mistaken, has at least that advantage. But, my dear brother, you will
find the weaker vessels a stumbling-block
and a constant thorn in the flesh of the
Christian pastor. Our sisters have a fatal
habit of mixing personal with religious feeling."

Here he sighed deeply, and Cyril suddenly
remembered a legend to the effect that the
Rev. George, in his curate days, possessed

a large cupboard full of unworn slippers worked by the faithful sisters of his flock. "Thinking that they love the manna furnished them by the faithful shepherd, they too often, and perhaps unconsciously, cherish a tenderness for the shepherd himself, and this leads to much that does not conduce to edifying. Such feelings are indeed harmless; but, though all things are lawful unto me, all things are not expedient, especially," he added, with unguarded confidence, " when one's wife is inclined to be jeal—— Well, you know, a young pastor should be prepared. And let no man be too sure of himself. Our poor sisters constantly want spiritual advice; let them seek it of an aged pastor. I would counsel you, whose manners and appearance are so strikingly calculated to impress weaker vessels with admiration, to confine your personal ministrations to men and elder sisters. You will be run after as a popular preacher, and women will be a snare to you, as tending to bring discredit on your calling, and giving occasion to the enemy to blaspheme. The Christian pastor must not only abstain from all evil, but from all appearance of evil—nay, the remotest suspicion of it. Our light has to shine strongly before men."

"I feel that most keenly," replied Cyril, roused to interest. "I feel that the lightest imputation upon us is absolutely fatal to our influence; that we are bound to a far stricter life than others. By the way, Everard, a very difficult case of conscience was submitted to our rector some years ago. There was a man doing good work in a parish consisting mainly of cultured and wealthy people, a man who had great personal influence. That man in early youth had done a wrong, which he bitterly repented, to atone for which he would have given years of his life —perhaps even life itself. A girl"—Cyril paused, and a thick, sobbing sigh caught his breath and impeded his utterance—"a girl had been, alas! led astray. She died by her own hand. Years after, when the penitent was in the height of his usefulness, a man

who had loved this girl found him out, and
attempted to avenge the unhappy girl's death
by killing him. He attacked him in a lonely
spot, on a ledge of narrow cliff." Cyril
paused again, and moistened his parched lips,
passing his handkerchief over his damp, chill
forehead at the same time. " There was a
struggle for life—no violence on the priest's
part; only the instinctive struggle for self-
preservation—and the would-be assassin was
hurled over the cliff to his death." Cyril
paused once more, and caught his breath
chokingly. " No suspicion was aroused; the
verdict was accidental death. The clergyman gave no evidence. He went on his
usual way, and no one ever guessed that his
hand—the hand which gave the sacred
elements !—had sent a fellow-creature to his
grave. The question which concerned our
rector was, whether the unintentional homicide
ought to have volunteered his evidence, and
confessed his involuntary share in the poor
creature's death. You see," continued Cyril,
suddenly lifting his face to his listener, " he

must have brought up the old scandal if
he had done so, and that, coupled with the
mystery about the death, would have utterly
ruined his career as a Christian pastor."

" True," replied George, thoughtfully
studying the intricacies of the Turkey carpet.
" How did your rector obtain possession of
these facts ? "

" The poor fellow confided in him—came to
him for advice in his trouble."

" And what was the advice ? "

" It was never given. Agitation of mind
brought on severe illness, which proved fatal.
The rector found it difficult to arrive at any
decision. What do *you* think ? "

" Truly, my dear young friend, the case is
perplexing. Had the question been referred
to me, I should certainly have made it a
matter of earnest prayer. As a mere abstract
question, I feel inclined to favour the erring
pastor's course of action. A revelation of
the truth would doubtless have given great
occasion to the enemy to blaspheme."

Cyril heaved a sigh of relief. " Very

true," he replied, sinking back into the depths of his easy-chair, whence he quickly started in nervous tremor as the door suddenly opened, and glanced apprehensively round, to see nothing more terrible than the bright face and light figure of Marion.

"Oh! here you are, you bad boys, looking as grave as two owls," she said, in her light, delicate treble. "George, your wife wants you in the drawing-room at once."

The obedient husband rose immediately, but paused lingeringly at the door. "We will discuss the matter further," he said. "Cyril and I have been having the most interesting conversation, Marion. I have passed a refreshing morning with him. We have more in common than I supposed."

And with an indulgent tap of his young sister's cheek, George vanished, and left the lovers alone, Marion charmed to find such harmony established between the two ecclesiastics, who bid fair at one time to differ as only those of the same creed under slightly varying aspects can differ.

"Isn't it provoking, Cyril?" she cried.
"Here is a telegram from Leslie, to say he
cannot spare time to come to-night, and
his regiment does not embark till the third.
If any one wants to wish him good-bye,
they can run over to Portsmouth to-morrow.
I dare say, indeed! The other officers are
coming; but we shall be short of men, I fear."

"Is that all?" returned Cyril, with a
sigh of relief; for he had turned pale and
shuddered at the sight of the telegram.
"Well, dearest, let us run over with your
father and Keppel to-morrow, and wish them
all good-bye at once. I rather envy the
admiral going on the Mediterranean station
at this murky season."

"You poor boy!" exclaimed Marion, placing
her hand upon his burning brow; "you look
as if you needed some kind of a change. I
am afraid your head is still aching."

"It is maddening," returned Cyril, detain-
ing the caressing hand. "To tell the truth,
I am very unwell. I ought not to have
walked this morning."

" Indeed you ought not. I saw that you were quite lame from fatigue."

" And who is to blame for my walk ?" returned Cyril, with forced gaiety; " who but Miss Everard ? I suppose I caught cold in Long's gig yesterday afternoon. I had no overcoat, meaning to walk. I feel as if I had been beaten all over."

" Poor dear ! " said Marion, tenderly. " And you actually have a little bruise here over the temple," she added, touching the place, which was tender even to her velvet touch.

" Oh, that's nothing ! " Cyril replied hastily; but he rose and approached a small mirror, into which he gazed apprehensively. " Ah yes, I dressed in a hurry, and hit myself with a hair-brush. And this," he added, pointing to a strip of plaster on his chin, " I did in shaving."

" What can we do for you ?" asked Marion. " I was going to ask you to carry some plants from the conservatory, but you must not."

" Come and sit by me, dear," Cyril replied, in his gracefully autocratic manner; " there is no anodyne like your presence."

So the lovers remained hand-in-hand by the library fire a good hour, Marion's bright eyes and caressing tones worshipping Cyril, who appreciated nothing so much as incense.

George Everard, in the mean time, was telling his wife what unexpected graces he had discovered in his future brother-in-law. " A very precious soul," he said. " He only needs Christian influence."

Mrs. Everard knew well that, according to the usage of her husband's tribe, the word Christian was not applicable to either of the Maitlands.

END OF VOL. I.

PRINTED BY WILLIAM CLOWES AND SONS, LIMITED, LONDON AND BECCLES.